Women of the Sun

Penguin Books

HYLLUS MARIS was born in Shepparton, Victoria, into the
Yorta Yorta tribe, the original inhabitants of the Murray
River area and traditional owners of that region. As a
child, she participated in the walk-out from a Government
Mission, the event that inspired the third story in this
book, *Nerida, the Waterlily*. A sociologist and prominent
activist in Aboriginal community development, she was
the founder of Worawa College, Frankston, the first
Aboriginal school in Victoria, and has initiated several
other Aboriginal organisations. Hyllus Maris has written
many poems and short stories and is researching a book
on Aboriginal history in Victoria.

SONIA BORG was born in Vienna, Austria, and studied
dramatic art in Germany after the second world war. In
1951 she moved to India and later she joined Shake-
speareana International, a theatre company that toured
throughout Asia. Arriving in Australia in 1961 she joined
Crawford Productions as drama coach, then became casting director and eventually a script editor and associate
producer. Now a freelance script writer, she has a
number of single plays for the Australian Broadcasting
Commission to her credit, and has also worked on the
series *Rush, Power Without Glory* and *I Can Jump
Puddles*. More recently she has adapted for the screen
Colin Thiele's books *Stormboy* and *Blue Fin*, and Frank
Dalby Davidson's *Dusty*.

Awards won by the original television mini-series *Women of the
Sun* include the 1982 United Nations Media Peace Prize, two
1983 Australian Writer's Guild awards, the Television Society of
Australia's award for best series script ('Alinta') and the main
drama award at the Canadian Banff Television Festival.

Women of the Sun

Hyllus Maris and Sonia Borg

Penguin Books

Penguin Books Australia Ltd,
487 Maroondah Highway, P.O. Box 257
Ringwood, Victoria, 3134, Australia
Penguin Books Ltd,
Harmondsworth, Middlesex, England
Penguin Books,
40 West 23rd Street, New York, N.Y. 10010, U.S.A.
Penguin Books Canada Ltd,
2801 John Street, Markham, Ontario, Canada
Penguin Books (N.Z.) Ltd,
Private Bag, Takapuna, Auckland 9, New Zealand

First published by Penguin Books Australia, 1985

Copyright © Hyllus Maris and Sonia Borg, 1985

Typeset in Century Old Style by Dudley E. King, Melbourne

Made and printed in Australia by
The Dominion Press–Hedges & Bell

CIP

Maris, Hyllus.
Women of the sun.

ISBN 0 14 007086 9.

I. Borg, Sonia, 1931–. II. Title.

A823'.3

Contents

Acknowledgements

Our thanks go to Mrs Geraldine Briggs, Mrs Margaret Tucker, and many other women who told us about their lives, and to whom we could always turn for help and advice.

Hyllus Maris
Sonia Borg

Towradgi

Towradgi was old. She was so old, no one remembered that there was once a time when she had been young. Her hair was the colour of the clouds; her skin, stretched tightly over ageing bones and criss-crossed with lines, was dark like the bark of a tree seared by fire. But, just as these ancient gum trees sprout new leaves because the devastation of the fire cannot destroy their spirit, and the life deep within, so there was under Towradgi's gnarled and time-toughened surface a great strength, and the resilience of youth. Across her upper arms and above her breasts cicatrices showed that she had been through the Law: she was a woman elder of the Nyari people. They had great power, these women elders. They had the knowledge that was handed down from the Ancestors who walked the earth at the beginning of creation.

She sat on a fallen log by the river, her cape of possum skin wrapped around her, for it was the time of year when the days are short, and the air crisp and cool. Next to her was a coolamon filled with herbs. Not far from her two young girls were gathering reeds for basket making, and roots for food.

They were Towradgi's pupils. As they grew up they would

learn from her many things: the use of herbs to cure pain and to heal wounds, to assist in childbirth, or to prevent conception. They would learn self-discipline, and the codes of conduct by which the people lived. They would learn about the mystery of creation, and their place in it. How much knowledge was given would depend on their ability to understand.

As Towradgi looked at Alinta, there was in her eyes, black like polished pebbles in their deep sockets, a gleam of satisfaction and of pride: she knew that Alinta would one day be her successor among the people. One day, Towradgi knew, she herself would die. The day still seemed far away, but it would come. It would come at a time when Alinta, the Flame, had been prepared to carry the torch of wisdom and of knowledge so that it could be passed on into the far distant future to those who would come after her.

It was peaceful down here by the river. A Murray cod was resting motionless in its home under a hollow log in the clear water, untroubled by the girls who were not here to catch fish. In the golden light of the autumn sun each blade of grass, each reed, each leaf, stood out clearly, filled with the mystery of its own growing.

Behind the river flats huge mountain ash rose from an abundance of smaller trees and undergrowth, and these, in turn, rose up between fallen and decaying logs and fallen branches which were covered in rich moss, and oozing moisture. Treeferns spread their quivering fronds into the rays of the sun that slanted between the eucalypts, and over small creeks and waterfalls.

High above Towradgi a wedgetailed eagle drew his circles in the sky. Towradgi knew that he was there; without looking up, she sent her spirit to soar with him, so that she could see from above the land her people had held in trust since time began. It stretched further than the eye could see: on one side it was bordered by the ocean, on the other its boundary grew faint in a haze on the horizon. There were rolling hills and golden plains where at this time of day the kangaroos would come to graze. The rivers and lakes were full of fish, and their banks and shores teemed with waterbirds: there were grey herons and white cranes, there were wild ducks and pelicans, and countless others. Trees and shrubs bore wild berries, and there were nourishing roots and plants.

Many times Towradgi had moved through this land with her people – from camp to camp, following the seasons, singing to the Ancestors who had left many signs of their passing: rocks, rivers, waterholes and mountains, places where their presence could be felt the moment one approached.

Soon Towradgi would take Alinta to one of them. Alinta, and her cousin Wonda. She would take them to the place that was sacred to the women. No men were allowed to set foot there. The time was coming when the two girls would enter womanhood. She would take them to the place where many generations of Nyari women had shed their first blood, and where many would go in time to come.

Towradgi's eyes turned to the two girls, whose brown bodies were slim like the reeds they were gathering. They were dressed in skirts made of emu feathers, and their hair fell to their shoulders, wavy like running water. They were talking to each other, laughing and giggling quietly. Towradgi could hear their voices, clear and sweet, like the sounds of birds.

And then a strange silence fell.

It was a silence no one could hear except Towradgi. It was absolute. It cut her off from the world around her, singled her out as someone who had to know.

Towradgi sat, alert. A wind sprang up. It ran across the reeds and made them tremble. It grew, and tore at branches, so that they shook with fear. It swept across the water, and the water shivered.

Towradgi rose to her feet and listened. She listened to the wind. He often would talk to her, tell her when the rain was coming, warn her of men approaching from a different tribe searching for women to take back with them. He was the messenger of things to come.

But on this day something was different.

This time there was a great fear in the wind himself. He came from a distant place, far beyond the land of the Nyari people and the neighbouring nations, and he spoke of things to come that could not be explained because there were no words for them.

3

The girls had straightened, their eyes on their old teacher who now stood erect, her chin held high, her eyes wide open, seeing into another time. With every fibre of her being she was trying to understand the message of the wind. In her mind's eye, Towradgi saw Alinta. She was different. She was older, and her eyes and hair were dull, as if she were a shadow of herself. She was running, dragging behind her a small girl. It seemed she did not know where to run, where to hide. Their bodies were covered in something that was flapping like peeling skin; skin that was decayed, unclean.

Behind them was the sea, grey and cold. Great breakers hit the shore. Then Towradgi saw the Hunter: it seemed to her that he had come from the Country of the Dead: his skin was pale, the colour of pipe clay. No living man looked like that. He carried in his hands a stick and when he raised it to his eye there was a flash of lightning and the crack of thunder. The image blurred, and Towradgi saw Alinta again, and once again she was a woman, not a child. She stood in a cloud of dust, as if there was a storm after a long drought, and her eyes were dark with rage. She spoke, but Towradgi could not understand what she said; she did not know the words. Once more Towradgi saw the land from above, from where the eagle flies, and she saw with a great shock that the land itself had changed. Gaping holes were torn into the belly of the earth; gone were almost all the trees and the grass, and the many creatures that lived in them. Much of the warm soil was cut off from the sun by large slabs of smooth, flat, stone. Huge rocks rose up from the hard ground, and she saw creatures were living in these rocks, like termites.

Towradgi, wise as she was, could not make sense of what she saw. All she knew was that the wind spoke of impending devastation and chaos, and that great suffering was coming to the people.

Her eyes turned to Alinta who squatted on the ground beside Wonda. Their eyes were on Towradgi, bewildered and frightened and awed by the old woman's strange expression.

The sun was about to set. In the bush the kookaburras began their defiant laughter. A chill was in the air. Soon night would come, and they had to hurry to the safety of their camp for it was dangerous to be in the bush after dark – a time when spirits were about, and when the earth itself could open up in front of you.

Towradgi felt a great wave of sorrow and compassion as she looked at the two young girls whose faces were full of the innocence of youth. How could she protect them from what was to come? How could she give them strength that would help their spirits to survive in the lives ahead of them?

She beckoned with her bony hand, and the girls came closer. Then she scooped up a handful of the dark river soil.

'Open your hands,' she said.

She put the soil firmly into their palms, and then closed their fingers over it. When she spoke her voice was loud and harsh, as if she spoke to all the future generations, and was challenging what was to come.

'Feel this earth,' she said. 'It is your flesh, your blood, your sinews. You are the earth, and the earth is you. Your ancestors were made from this earth, and this earth is sacred. Whatever happens, remember that.'

A l i n t a,
the Flame

A s they hurried back through the bush, the girls now and then looked anxiously at their tutor, but the old woman strode in silence, swinging her digging stick, and keeping her vision to herself. What was to come, would come.

Alinta soon forgot the incident by the river. She was happy. She was learning many things from Towradgi, from her mother Kiah, from her aunt Warroo, who often chuckled mysteriously and had a twinkle in her eye when she looked at Alinta, whose childbody was beginning to change into that of a young woman. Alinta and the women would set out together to harvest food – roots, berries, plants; they would catch echidnas, lizards, bandicoots, all of which made good eating when roasted between hot stones underneath a fire. There would be much gossiping and laughter, and sometimes serious discussions about women's business: who would marry whom, and how so-and-so had received a hiding from her husband because she had made eyes at another man; or how one of them had argued when she had been accused of being tardy in her duties.

She learnt from Towradgi – she and Wonda – that the world was divided into two moieties: *Pund-jel* and *Pal-ly-an.*

Everything that lived – man, plant, animal – belonged to one or other of these groups. They were divided once again, and it was not easy to remember who was to marry whom according to the Law, who was 'of the right skin'. It was of great importance that the Law was followed; it made sure that humans lived in harmony with one another, and with the world around them.

Alinta was Pund-jel, a child of the sun. This knowledge filled her with pride and pleasure. Her friends – her totems – were amongst others the eagle, the blue crane, the crimson rosella. When she saw them flying through the sky, or when she heard their call, she felt good, secure: she belonged with them, and they with her; they had their place in the great scheme of things.

Winter came, bringing cold winds and rain. The Nyari sat together, huddled in their capes of possum fur, telling each other stories of times when animals had been human, of heroes and warriors, of evil spirits, of the feats of hunters. Alinta saw the land disappear in mist and clouds that wafted through the bush like living things, till she and the people seemed alone in a world of nothingness. The camp dogs came close to the fires which struggled to keep alight because the wood was moist; at night Alinta would share her bed of dry grass and leaves with her favourite pup. Then slowly the closest trees would re-emerge, standing black in the transparent grey, and the sun would break through, and millions of drops would sparkle in her rays. The days grew longer. The People moved to set up camp close to the sea. The men prepared their bark canoes because soon the fish would be plentiful.

One day, as Alinta and Wonda were sitting with Towradgi on a fallen log, learning which herb would cure thinning hair, which was good for healing wounds, a soft breeze came up. Alinta felt it touch her hair like a caress, and the thin branches of a young eucalypt swayed gently to and fro. There was something special about that breeze, and Alinta was very still. A honey bee came and sat briefly on her arm. Alinta watched it till it flew away, then cast a quick glance at Towradgi, aware that she had her eyes on her. She was wondering if these were the signs of someone's coming, someone who had a greeting just for her.

There was a slight smile in Towradgi's eyes – like the old have for those who are just setting out.

'Soon you'll be a woman now,' she said, 'a woman of the Nyari people. You be proud of that.'

As they went back to camp they came across the footprints of a man. They were unrecognisable and they knew he was not one of the clan. Wonda was immediately fearful. She was one who loved listening, wide-eyed, to the stories of ghosts and weird creatures that the grown-ups told around the fires, and then she imagined she saw them everywhere in the bush. Now she expected to be confronted by one of them any moment.

Alinta, too, was filled with some trepidation, but she saw that the stranger had made no attempt to conceal himself, and so it was unlikely that he had come with an evil purpose. He must be a visitor. Her heart gave a small leap: could he be the one who had sent signs of his coming? The blood rushed to her cheeks.

When they arrived at the camp at last, there was on top of a high dune the figure of a man. He stood, outlined against the evening sky, immobile, for all to see. There he would wait until invited to join the people down below; that was the custom.

Alinta stopped in her tracks, eyes fixed on him. Then she heard Towradgi's voice, and she spoke calmly, but with satisfaction: 'So he has come; the one who is to be your husband.'

It was Murra, the West Wind.

Alinta forgot Wonda and Towradgi; clasping her coolamon filled with herbs, she ran to where her mother was roasting yams in the fire. There she crouched, and she was suddenly like a small, frightened animal. She did not want to leave her people. She wanted to stay with those she loved and who loved her.

'Mother,' she said, 'why has he come? Why is he here?'

Kiah looked at her daughter, and she remembered how she had felt when she was a child and had seen her promised husband. 'He is your husband according to the Law,' she said, 'but it will be a long time before he takes you to his people . . .'

Alinta looked up, and she felt awe at what lay ahead, and then there mingled with her fear a strange kind of longing for that distant figure on the dune.

Aunt Warroo came from where she had been busy by her fire, and she chuckled with pleasure and excitement. 'Look at her,' she said, 'look at Alinta! Alinta, the Flame, and Murra, the West Wind . . . what a fire there will be!'

Two women were now on their way to welcome Murra. They carried fruits and roasted fish in their coolamons, and Alinta could hear their voices as they called out to him. She watched entranced, everything else forgotten.

Warroo had sat down by the fire while her own yams burnt to cinder. 'Ah,' she said, 'when I think of the time before I married . . . How handsome was Morrorra!' She raised her arms and flapped them: 'I was like a young brolga then, that's what Morrorra said.' Alinta looked at her: how she had changed! She was more like an echidna now, squat and solid, and her hair stood up like spikes.

Soon it was dark. Their campfires burnt in the vastness of the night. Murra sat with Alinta's father and her brother, and with two other Elders, one of whom was Warroo's husband. The first excitement about Murra's visit had died down, and everybody went about their business – cooking, eating, sharpening spear heads for the next day's hunt. Dogs walked about collecting their share of food, or lay asleep by the fires.

Alinta watched Murra from the shadows behind her father's mia-mia. He was more handsome than she remembered. When she had seen him first she was only little, and marriage happened to other people. But now! Would it be hard to be a woman? She suddenly wished time would stop and she could stay a child. She knew what marriage meant, and the thought of a man entering her body frightened her, yet at the same time made her wonder. And she would have a child grow in her; would it hurt? There was much talk about such things among the women; some of them suffered, others didn't.

She looked for Wonda, and they sat together and furtively watched how Murra unwrapped the presents he had made. Her father looked very pleased. She wondered if Murra would be kind. If she made mistakes, would he punish her? Some of the men were quick to beat their women. If he did, she would run away and come back to her own people. Wonda agreed with her.

Her promised husband had been killed in a skirmish with another tribe, and now she was to be married to the dead man's brother. Still, nothing was yet settled.

Murra handed a stone axe to Turuga, Alinta's father, and it was much admired as it was passed around. Murra looked strong and powerful; the light of the fire reflected in his eyes, and his skin gleamed with health and vigour. He liked to laugh, and his teeth were white – like foam from the sea. Alinta felt suddenly she would like to be very close to him. It was a strange, pleasant feeling, and she savoured it.

'Aunt Warroo says he is a great warrior and hunter,' she said at last. There was a pause. It was as if Wonda could read her thoughts.

'He is handsome,' she said. Alinta was pleased.

'Do you think so?' she asked quickly, and then, without waiting for an answer: 'I think so, too . . .' For a few more moments she looked at him, and then she said with growing satisfaction, 'He is a dancer, and a maker of songs . . .'

Murra had unwrapped a necklace of eucalyptus seeds, and the men laughed and teased him about who was to wear it. Then Alinta's brother spotted his young sister, and Murra got to his feet and came towards Alinta.

The moment Alinta realized that he knew where she was, she lowered her face and wished the earth would swallow her. Yet at the same time there was nothing she wished more than to meet with him. She saw his feet as he stopped in front of her, then heard his voice. It was a gentle voice. 'I have brought you a special gift, Alinta,' he said softly.

Alinta did not move. She could not, even if she had wanted to. She forgot to breathe. Wonda watched in silence.

'Will you take it?'

Alinta raised her head, eyes still lowered to the ground. Murra let the string of seeds slip around her neck. She felt it touch her skin, and she decided straight away that she would always wear it, never part with it.

Murra stood for another moment, not sure what to say to this bride who was still a child. But he saw that she was beautiful.

He walked back to the men and Alinta watched him go, and

she let out her breath. She shot a quick glance at Wonda, and Wonda giggled. Alinta's face lit up, and she felt a great surge of joy and pride. If marriage was to be, she was glad it was Murra who would be her husband.

That night Alinta lay awake for a long time. The day had been warm and humid, but after dark cold gusts began to blow from the sea, and soon the surf was pounding against the shore. The camp was sheltered by a huge cliff that jutted up into the sky, and Alinta felt protected, safe, in her family's mia-mia which was made of boughs and leaves and thick grass and reeds. She could hear the voices of her parents as they talked quietly in the dark. She could not understand what they were saying, but she was sure they were talking about Murra and her future. Murra, who would now be in the area where the young unmarried men had their place, perhaps even now taking his turn to guard the camp at night.

Next morning, as Alinta walked along the beach followed by her small brother Neer-wun and her cousin Tulla, she felt important and grown-up. She imagined herself as mother, and as she went about collecting mussels she called out to the boys, teaching them a thing or two, and scolding them if they were not attentive.

Clouds drifted across the sky after the night's storm. The sea was still restless, and there were crests of white foam as the breakers rolled ashore. Seagulls uttered their piercing cries as they swooped from the sky, and a redbill walked about on long thin legs, searching, pecking, now and then looking at the children with knowing eyes. It was one of little Tulla's totems and had to be treated with respect. In the far distance Alinta could still see a small group of women outlined against the crisp blue of the sea and the pure, clean sand, collecting mussels, like herself.

Then Alinta noticed something strange: something on the water's edge. Some creatures were lying on the sand, and the retreating tide still licked around them so that she did not know if they were moving of their own accord, or if it was the water playing with what seemed like loose flaps of skin.

Alinta stood, not sure what it was she saw. Was it some large fish that had died and had been washed ashore? She felt a tingling on the scalp. Should she venture closer? Further up the beach the two boys were still throwing their toy spears to see who was the strongest.

She summoned her courage and cautiously moved closer, ready to turn and run at any moment. And then she could see what it was, and her hair almost stood up in fright, in horror. She stood transfixed, unable to believe her eyes.

The creatures had heads, arms, legs, like men. But they had no real colour. Their eyes were shut, and they seemed dead. But then one of them moved slightly, and for a moment Alinta saw the eyes of one of them open. She had seen the eyes of fish that had that colour: a faint grey-blue. Who were they? Where did they come from? Had they lain on the bottom of the sea and been brought up by the storm the night before? They were spirits. No human being looked like that. They were spirits from the Country of the Dead. They had come to haunt the living; they brought death with them.

The two boys had followed her and now stood, eyes wide, fists crammed into their mouths. Alinta grabbed them by their arms and turned them away, and they all ran back to the camp, almost flying across the sand. When they could see the people, they began to scream their terror: 'Monsters! There are monsters by the sea! Evil spirits! Spirits from the Country of the Dead!'

Soon a group of warriors, spears at the ready, were on their way to where the children pointed.

Alinta and the children, still shivering, stayed behind with the women; there was fear and consternation and bewilderment among those who waited. What did it mean? What was it the children had discovered? Would the men be able to defend themselves against such beings? They looked at Towradgi who listened to the description Alinta gave.

'So they have come,' she said at last, and turned and walked away to be alone.

When the men returned they had the two creatures in their midst, half dragging, half carrying them. Now that Alinta was with the others, she had the courage to study them more carefully: their skin, pale like pipe-clay, was blistered and in parts exposed the flesh. One of them had hair that stood around his head like dead grass; the other's was more like fire. Something hung around their bodies. At first Alinta thought that it was skin; it was different from anything she had ever seen.

Now everybody talked at once, asking questions, not waiting for an answer, calling out in astonishment at the sight. Then Turuga, Alinta's father, raised his hand and commanded silence. 'These', he said, 'are men, not spirits. Murra has heard of them before.'

The men let the creatures slide to the ground, where they sat and looked about in fear. The people saw that their eyes were red and inflamed, and that they seemed nearly blind. Their lips were cracked, their hair caked with salt. One of them whimpered as he crouched. A strange smell came from them – like rotten fish.

Then Murra told how he had heard that the people of the Yarra-Yarra tribe had found men of this kind. Numbers of them had come in big canoes, so the rumour went, and they had settled in areas near the sea. No one knew where their country was, and why they had not stayed at home.

The elders decided that they were to be given food and water. Perhaps after they had eaten it would be possible to talk to them, to hear their story. The two strangers ate so greedily that they were sick, and when Turuga finally questioned them as to who they were, and why they had entered the land of the Nyari without permission, they did not understand a word, but spoke to each other in low voices, and stared about. One of them, the one with hair like fire, tried to smile to show his gratitude.

Alinta had never seen grown men behave like this; filled with revulsion and unease, she wondered what their coming meant, and whether they would soon leave again. She also felt some pity: it was clear that they were desperate because they were in a strange country, far away from home, from their families.

That evening, when the strangers had been put into a mia-mia with guards on either side of it, the elders discussed what was to be done with them. Towradgi had kept silent until now, but at last she spoke, and her voice was loud and strident so that everyone could hear:

'We don't want them here,' she said. 'They will bring great suffering to the people.'

There was a brief silence; then Turuga said, 'They are weak and sick, how can they harm us, sister? They are helpless, we are strong. Why should we be afraid?'

Alinta looked at her father. He was calm, confident. She admired him. It seemed he knew no fear.

Morrorra and the other elders agreed with him. 'Let us keep them till they are fit and well, and then we shall send them back to their own country.'

'Let us do that,' Turuga said. 'If we were lost in a far country, we would hope the people there would do the same to us.'

Towradgi said nothing more. She saw the men were compassionate. Perhaps they were curious, too. Perhaps they wanted to find out more about these men who were so different.

But there was one more thing she had to say: 'Don't let them walk near the women.' That was all. She could not explain to anyone the message of the wind.

The two men of clay were given names: Man-from-the-Sea, and Hair-of-Fire. A guard kept constant watch over them, and the people once more went about their business: the men hunting, fishing; the women gathering fruit and vegetables. They shared their food with their uninvited guests who soon grew well and strong.

They found that Hair-of-Fire was likeable enough. On the first morning of their stay he had tried to speak to his guards, pointing at himself and his companion, smacking his lips, pretending he was drinking. When they brought him water in a coolamon he heard them say the word '*wyuna*' and he repeated it many times between swallowing, and he laughed and bowed; he was so happy to be understood that his guards began to laugh with him. Soon he made friends with the children, and he drew pictures in the sand of strange animals, and spoke their names in his own language – strange sounds: 'horse', 'cow', and 'pig'. He called the dingoes 'dogs' and when the children repeated what he said he was very pleased. He sat on the beach and sang songs which made him sad; his eyes filled with tears, and he looked across the sea with longing.

Sometimes Murra and he would walk together, and Murra showed him many things. Often Hair-of-Fire would break into cries of delight when he saw the beauty of the land, and he would scrape handfuls of soil together and look at it with admiration. Once Murra saw him kneel in front of two sticks he had tied together, and he was murmuring quietly, eyes closed. There was something in his manner that made Murra think he was talking to the Great Spirit Baiame.

Man-from-the-Sea was not like that. He did not care about the children, and he watched the men through narrow and suspicious eyes. Sometimes he would argue wildly with his companion, and it would look as if he was about to strike him savagely with his fist. After that he would sit in sullen silence.

They made no sign to leave, and the elders decided it was time they did. They called them, and in simple words explained that they were now well enough to return to their own people. 'Your families must worry about you,' Turuga said, 'and you, too, must think of them . . .' He handed them a basket containing food for their journey.

At first the two men stared, bewildered. Then, realizing what the elders meant, they were desperate. They hastily talked with one another, then Hair-of-Fire summoned all his meagre knowledge of the language, and when he could not find the words, made frantic signs. He patted the ground in front of him, and he said 'We stay! We stay! We good warriors!' He grabbed a spear and leapt about, as if fighting enemies. Man-from-the-Sea looked from him to the elders and back again, fiercely wanting them to understand. Then, dissatisfied with his companion's efforts, he spoke harshly, imploringly, in his own language, grabbing his own throat with his hands as if strangling himself. Finally, he seized Hair-of-Fire, tore the ragged cover off his back, and pointed at a mass of scars that criss-crossed from the shoulders to the waist.

The elders and all those around watched in puzzled silence. What was the meaning of these scars? The back of this man must once have been like one open wound. Did he receive these injuries in a battle? Were they cicatrices, showing that he had passed an initiation? If so, why was he ashamed of them? For that he was: he quickly pulled away and tried to hide his back.

One thing the elders understood: their guests did not want to leave.

They discussed this, and they called Towradgi. She remained adamant: 'The women are uneasy; they don't trust these men. They have no families with them, they have different customs. They are like children who know nothing, yet they have the strength of men.'

Turuga nodded. 'We have talked about this, sister. If they are to stay, they must go through the Law. They must become men in spirit. There is no other way.'

Towradgi snorted. She did not believe the two would pass the test because going through the Law meant to have discipline and courage.

Morrorra agreed with Turuga and the other elders. They looked at the old woman who shook her head impatiently. 'Send them away,' she said. 'Their staying will bring great sorrow.'

'How can it, sister, if they obey the Law?'

'You are blind! You cannot see the danger!'

The elders decided that they would teach the strangers. If they did not learn, they would be sent away. Slowly, patiently, they were shown the simplest things: what food to eat, what to avoid. They were taught the names of things; they were given a place in the clan, and their tribal mothers, fathers, sisters, brothers, were pointed out to them.

They were taken out to hunt, and the men found that they did not know how to throw a spear, or a throwing stick; they did not know how to read tracks, how to walk soundlessly through the bush, and even after they had been shown these things, they failed to learn. Once, while stalking a mob of kangaroos, the men stopped and conversed by signs as to who would spear which kangaroo. Just then Man-from-the-Sea stepped on a pebble and let out a yell of pain that sent the kangaroos skipping. Morrorra, whose mouth had watered at the thought of the delicious meal, lost his temper. 'You fool!' he shouted, 'with you here we shall starve!' And they had to start their search from the beginning.

That evening, Morrorra, his anger gone, mimicked Man-from-the-Sea. Morrorra was getting on in years, but he was agile like a youngster. All the people were assembled around their fires; there had been some story-telling, and the accounts of the day were given. Morrorra hopped around on one foot, clutching the other one in his hand. 'And this is how they hunt!' he called, and everybody rolled about with mirth. Alinta looked at Man-from-the-Sea: he was the only one who did not laugh.

Man-from-the-Sea liked to hunt. He wanted to excel. He spent long days practising to throw spear and woomera. One day Alinta and Wonda were sitting by the water, weaving baskets for Towradgi, when they saw him coming. A blue crane had given them company on the far side of the pond, walking about with slow dignity, picking this and that at the water's edge and then standing motionless in a spot of sunlight. Now it stretched its neck and flapped its wings to fly away. Man-from-the-Sea killed it with his throwing stick. He picked up the dead bird by its slender neck, swinging it as he walked back to camp to show how skilful he had been. He did not look at the two girls who sat horrified and silent, but he was sure they admired him. From that moment on Alinta hated him: the blue crane had been her friend; it was one of her totems.

As they foraged together for roots, the women discussed the two pale strangers. They wondered how they could be so igno- rant. How could they have looked after their women and their children? They were useless. Perhaps that was the reason why they had been sent away? Banished. Aunt Warroo chuckled: what a song and dance she'd make if Morrorra failed to provide for her and her children! She, too, would send him away to a far land. Alinta listened silently, and she thought of Murra. He would protect her. He would fight for her. With him close by she need not fear the likes of Man-from-the-Sea.

One morning she and Towradgi sat by the sea. The clouds were low but had begun to dissolve into a fine mist, diffused by the rays of the rising sun. There was a gentle swell, and the shore was lost in infinity.

An eagle flew above, wings outstretched and motionless, soaring and gliding with the wind.

Alinta's heart was full. The world was beautiful beyond description. She glanced at Towradgi and found to her surprise that the old woman's eyes were shut. Alinta looked at the many lines in Towradgi's face, at the gnarled hands, the white hair. 'Yarmuk', she said in a hushed voice, 'are you asleep?'

Towradgi grunted; 'I am thinking.'

Alinta was filled with reverence. 'You know everything.'

'See the eagle flying?' Towradgi said, her eyes remaining shut. 'He knows everything. He is the messenger of the Great Spirit. He has been here since time began; he will be here when everything is gone.'

Towradgi had always been a thorough teacher, but now – since the men with faces like pipe-clay had come – she was more urgent in her instruction, as if she were preparing the girls for battle. Towradgi knew that a person can bear anything, as long as you know yourself, and have self-respect.

She taught them how at the beginning of creation the earth had been flat and in darkness, and how the Great Spirit Baiame sent the sun to give light, and how Pund-jel made man, Pal-ly-an woman; how they were made out of the earth and the sea; and how the Ancestors, great spiritual beings, walked over the flat land and created rivers, mountains, lakes. All this she taught, and many other things, things secret to the women.

The days passed, and the nights, and summer came. Most of the land was dry. It was the time when the Nyari moved higher into the hills where creeks never ceased to flow in shaded gullies, where there were groves of satinwood, blackwood, and tree ferns. In the clearings the grass stayed green, fed by the moisture that drifted from the sea and was caught between the mountain tops.

Hair-of-Fire had learnt many things. Turuga and the other elders were very pleased with him. He now dressed like the men, and his skin had become darker; it was no longer the colour of a fledgeling without feathers, but rather like the inside of a tree, a pale golden brown. Already he could speak the language well, and after a day's hunt he would sit with the other men around the fire, sharpening his spears, listening to their stories, and even telling some of his own. Sometimes he would draw pictures in the sand of the mia-mias his people built, and of the large canoes that could carry many men and were blown across the sea by the wind. It seemed he had lived on a tiny piece of land on which grew nothing except rocks and stones, and that his mother, father, brothers, sisters often had no food. So he took from those who had plenty, and for this the elders of his country had banished him. Him, like many others. When he spoke of his countrymen he became bitter and shook his head: it seemed that many had done evil things and he said he was glad he was not with them.

Wonda and Alinta often sat and listened to his stories, the dogs lying at their feet. Alinta was proud that her father had entrusted Murra with much of the responsibility of teaching Hair-of-Fire. She noticed that Wonda often looked at Hair-of-Fire, and that when he noticed her she grew bashful and ran away to hide.

'Do you like him?' Alinta asked, not sure this could be possible.

'I like his hair,' Wonda said evasively, 'it's special.'

Man-from-the-Sea was to be sent away. The elders saw that he could hunt and fend for himself, but that he did not belong to them. He did not want to learn their customs, he did not join in their dancing and their singing; he kept to himself. He was inexplicable. His spirit was dark and without capacity for joy.

The women feared him and kept away from him. Alinta noticed him watching her hungrily. Not only her, but others. It was strange: no other man ever made her feel so afraid, so conscious of herself, so uneasy. She could guess his thoughts and knew how dangerous he was. She was glad he would be sent away, but she was worried that he would return and haunt the camp like an evil spirit. It would be impossible for her and the other women to go about free and unafraid as they had done before he had come to them.

One afternoon Alinta and Conara were by the river, fishing. Conara was the daughter of Kiah's sister, Alinta's cousin. She was a cheerful, happy woman, mother of a small boy. She knew that once again a spirit child had entered her to return into the world. Alinta, her coolamon full, made to return to her mother who was with the other women not far away, sitting in the shade and weaving dilly bags. As she passed some ferns she caught a glimpse of Man-from-the-Sea among the rocks nearby. She thought of turning back to warn Conara who had stayed behind to bathe in the cool water, but she was afraid of having perhaps to face him on her own. Rather, she ran to tell the other women. She had just reached them when she heard Conara scream. It was a wild, dreadful scream, and then there was silence.

The women grabbed their digging sticks and ran to Conara's rescue. Alinta followed, ashamed that she had failed her cousin.

Man-from-the-Sea was trying to subdue Conara. He had his hands around her throat in a desperate attempt to silence her. She still struggled feebly, trying to kick and claw. The women struck Man-from-the-Sea with their fists and their digging sticks, and the air was filled with their screams and shouts of anger and abhorrence. The whole bush around them was in uproar: cockatoos screeched as they wheeled above, and many other birds uttered their warning cries.

Man-from-the-Sea had let go of Conara to defend himself. Alinta ran to her and saw the marks on her throat, saw she was near death from shock and fright.

Then the men came and took Man-from-the-Sea back to camp.

He knew he would be put to death, and he was terrified. He pleaded with Hair-of-Fire to speak for him, explain that he had meant no harm. It was natural for a man to want a woman, he pleaded. Hair-of-Fire turned away. He feared for his own life, and he had grown sick and tired of his countryman whose manner was a constant threat to his own safety.

All the people assembled to see justice done. Hair-of-Fire sat with them, but he did not look at Man-from-the-Sea. He could not. Man-from-the-Sea was held by two warriors, and he was sick with fear.

Towradgi sat among the women, erect, her eyes burning like black flames. Alinta was next to her, and the old woman's hand was on her arm.

Turuga stood up and faced Man-from-the-Sea, pointing at him. 'Man-from-the-Sea,' he said, 'You have broken our trust.

How can a man do such a thing to his sister! You have offended us and the Ancestors! We were ready to take you and make you part of ourselves. You have disgraced your clan and your people. You have learnt nothing. You are no more one of us. It is finished.'

A swarm of black cockatoos flew overhead and screeched.

Turuga handed him a narrow shield. 'Take this and defend yourself.' Man-from-the-Sea grabbed it, and then stood trembling. He looked about, but there was no help anywhere. He was alone, an outcast. Alinta, like the others, felt no pity. He was better dead.

A warrior rose to his feet, spear ready. Hair-of-Fire tried to turn away, but Morrorra forced him to look on. 'See what happens when the Law is broken,' he said, and his face was grim.

The warrior hurled his spear, but Man-from-the-Sea dodged sideways. He screamed in terror. He did not want to die. Keri, Alinta's brother, now stood up. 'Is this the man you are?' he called with contempt. Man-from-the-Sea fell to his knees, and Keri's spear hit the tree above his head. Then Morrorra rose, and he was very calm. 'I shall not miss.' And he flung his spear, and he killed Man-from-the-Sea.

After that the people moved to another place because of the evil that had happened, and that would linger on.

Not much later Murra went back to his own people, and though Alinta had not talked much with him, she missed him. She missed seeing him return from the hunt, or sitting by the fire, and she often thought of him.

But then Alinta's and Wonda's initiation was approaching, and there was much preparation. When at last the time had come, she, Wonda, Towradgi, Warroo and Conara set out for the area which was sacred to the women. They travelled through it many days, singing to the spirits that lived in trees and rocks, announcing to them why they had come. It seemed to Alinta as if she could hear their answer in the rustling of the leaves, and it was as if many eyes were watching as the small group moved along. Each bird, each animal, each living thing, took on a special significance in this place. High above them she sensed rather than saw the wedgetailed eagle flying. She thought of Murra and the many things Towradgi had taught her and Wonda, and she felt as if she was part of life itself. A small part, but important, and eternal.

Until now, Alinta and Wonda had not been allowed to see the site which had been the place of initiation for many generations of Nyari women. It was a strange place, heavy with mystery; a place where close to the beginning of creation ancestral beings, huge and powerful, had sat down and made camp, and had infused some of their own power into the oval rocks which rose abruptly and bare from the ground. Their power was also in the river that ran between the rocks; it never ran dry, even in the longest drought. The power here would give fertility to the Nyari women. Fertility and health and strength to them and to their children.

The women knew what to do and went about their business swiftly and without fuss. They cleaned the site and strengthened the mia-mia in which the two girls would be staying for the coming days. They collected food and soon were settled. Then Alinta's and Wonda's bodies were painted with sacred signs that were full of meaning, and the days passed filled with mystery; there was much chanting, singing, talking to the spirits. Alinta felt as if her mind was floating in a sea of time where there was no past, no present, and she was very close to the Ancestors. And her body bled to show its ripeness.

After Alinta's and Wonda's initiation was complete and they returned to the camp, the young men gave their pledge that they would protect and honour them. There was a celebration with dancing, singing, feasting. Alinta was proud and happy. She was a woman now. A woman of the Nyari people.

So was Wonda.

It had been decided by the elders that Wonda would become the wife of Hair-of-Fire. It was known he had a wife and child in his former country, but he could never return to them, and it was necessary for him to have a family to make his new life complete as a man of the Nyari.

He had been taught many things: not only self-discipline – how to bear pain and thirst and hunger; he had also been shown the meaning of the sacred stones and signs – symbols of the mysteries of creation, and sources of power of the people. As time would pass, he would learn more. They had made him a man of the Nyari, and they trusted him.

There was much talk about the forthcoming marriage among the women, and they thought he would make a tolerable husband.

He himself seemed very pleased at the thought of marrying Wonda, and he would catch her eye and smile at her, and she would smile back at him – shyly, bashfully.

The seasons passed. The Nyari moved across the land they held in trust, and Hair-of-Fire learnt about all the places that were significant and sacred; he learnt about the springs and waterholes where no man must drink even during drought so that there was water for the animals to survive. He learnt how to tend the bush with fire during certain times of the year, so that the grass would grow more luscious the next season.

Then, one day, Murra returned to claim Alinta.

Turuga stood in front of them. 'Murra,' he said, 'are you ready for your trial of self-discipline before marriage?' Murra said yes. Alinta, too, was asked, and said yes.

Around them were all the others – men, women, children, ready to see them off. Hair-of-Fire was there, as was Wonda. They too would soon have to pass this test: to live together for three months in the bush, yet not to lie with each other during all this time.

Alinta was dressed in her cape of possum fur and skirt of emu feathers. She wore a headband around her hair, and she carried her coolamon, dilly bag and digging stick. Around her neck was the string of eucalyptus seeds Murra had given her. These were all the things she owned.

Towradgi's eyes were on her, stern, but filled with affection and pride. Alinta was her favourite pupil. Over the past years she had learnt many things, but she also had an ability to sense how others felt, a gentleness towards all living creatures, something that could not be taught. And there was about her a vitality, and courage, and an exuberance which sparkled in her eyes and burst forth in laughter.

Just now she stood demurely next to Murra, eyes on the ground, heart beating fast, wondering what lay ahead.

When later they walked through the bush, Murra, carrying his spears, his woomera, his waddy, stone knife and stone axe, led the way. She followed silently, aware only of herself and of her future husband. Everything else seemed a blur. Neither could think of anything to say.

He wondered what she thought. Was she pleased to become his wife? He pictured the time when she would meet his own people. He was glad it was Alinta and no one else who was to be his wife according to the Law. A man could be burdened with a woman he didn't care for much; not all of them were lovely like Alinta – cheerful and beautiful and spirited. He had seen her grow like a flower. It would be hard to obey the Law and not take her sweet body in his arms.

There was a rustling in the bush. He snapped out of his thoughts and, sensing danger, grabbed his spear, gesturing to Alinta to stay back. They both stood motionless, ears pricked.

Silence. Nothing, except the shrill, even whistle of a bird.

Their unseen enemy must be close by, waiting, watching. Who was he? Alinta's flesh began to crawl, her scalp to tingle. Murra stood, eyes scanning the bush, ready to face any danger. 'Who's there?' he called.

A wombat scuttled from the undergrowth, plump and hairy, intent on its own business.

Murra grinned sheepishly and cast a sideways glance at Alinta. What would she think of him! How foolish he must look! He, the great warrior and hunter, had been challenging a wombat!

Alinta giggled, and her eyes danced with mirth. Kookaburras started cackling in the trees above and filled the air with their raucous laughter. Murra too began to laugh. They looked at one another, and went on laughing, not just about the wombat but about the beauty of life itself, and the joy of being with each other.

When it grew dark they set up camp. A windbreak was constructed. Alinta had dug up some roots, picked some berries; Murra had killed two ducks.

27

Alinta twirled firesticks in dry moss and grass, and Murra watched. At last smoke appeared, then a small flame leapt up and was fanned by the wind, so that it began to lick hungrily at leaves and twigs. Soon it would spread like a living thing, and keep away the darkness, the evil spirits, the strange creatures, neither human nor animal, that live in the bush and come out at night.

'See how the wind plays with the flames?' Murra asked in a low voice.

Alinta nodded.

'That's me, my namesake, Murra the West Wind; he knows I'm here . . .'

Alinta smiled, and the breeze touched her hair, her face.

'See how he makes the flames dance? That's you, Alinta. You are the fire . . .'

Alinta did not know what to say; her heart was pounding, the blood rushed through her veins. Murra chuckled softly.

'Where does the fire go, Alinta?'

Alinta tossed back her head and answered pertly: 'You tell me where it comes from, I'll tell you where it goes.'

The moon had not yet risen; the stars were very bright, and it was as if they were dancing in the sky. Alinta thought of the story Towradgi had told her and Wonda, the story of Priepriggie, the hunter and songman who was much loved by his people. He provided them with everything they needed: by day he would hunt for them so that they were never hungry; at night he sang for them so that they could dance to his music. One day as he hunted flying foxes, the foxes flew up and seized him, and carried him into the sky. The people missed him greatly; they did not know where he had gone, and they mourned for him. But when they looked up into the sky at night they saw that the stars that had been in chaos until then were dancing to his music, and were in harmony because of him.

It was not easy for Murra and Alinta to obey the Law. Who but themselves would have known that they had broken it? But the Nyari were taught not to lie, and it would have been against their pride. At the end of the three months they would be questioned by the elders, and they would have to tell the truth. They knew they had to be masters of themselves, their passions, if the people were to survive.

One afternoon, close to the end of the trial period, they were making for the river where Murra was going to spear some fish. They were at ease with each other, having talked about many things, and having been through long spells of silence.

They heard the dingo howl. It was strange that he should call at this time of day, and this time of the year. His eerie call was full of sorrow and despair; it echoed back from the surrounding bush so that the whole country seemed filled with it. Then there was a crack of thunder, though there were no clouds in sight, and then silence.

Alinta and Murra looked at one another: the sound of thunder had come from the direction of the river which they could see flowing swiftly and quietly behind a group of dark, slender trees. Still affected by what they had heard, and not sure if they should investigate, they became aware of something else: a regular splashing, creaking sound, and a human voice calling out in a chant-like way. Gradually the sounds came closer.

Suddenly a large canoe appeared around the bend in the river. Six men were in it: two were rowing, one was sitting at the end, scanning the surrounding countryside, another was trailing a piece of string; it was he who was singing out as he pulled something from the water and dropped it back again.

All these were men with faces like pipe-clay, but there were two more, and they were not. Their skin was dark, their hair black – they were of the people, but from another nation. They were dressed like the strangers: all of them had their bodies covered in many colours, and on their heads they wore something similar to coolamons upside down which kept their eyes in the shade. The two black men had something in their hands that looked like strangely shaped, polished clubs.

Alinta and Murra did not move; they were invisible, part of the landscape to those who passed. They stared at the unexpected sight as it glided along, oars rising, dipping, rising, dipping, moving smoothly, insidiously, inexorably ... carrying these aliens from another world on the clear water of the river, past the majestic trees – blue gum and manna gum – and the high grass and reeds that whispered in the wind.

Long after the boat had passed and the sounds had died Alinta and Murra did not speak. Then Murra decided to challenge the intruders.

They knew how the river curved, and so they cut across the land. Murra walked ahead, the blood now running hotly in his veins, spurred on by indignation, outrage. Alinta followed silently, on the one hand admiring his courage, on the other thinking it might be better to go back to camp which was not far away. What if Murra and she were killed? Who would warn the others?

When they once more caught sight of the strangers the boat had been moored to a dead tree, and three of the men were unloading it. The one who seemed to be the leader sat on a fallen log and watched the others, now and then pointing out where they should put the things they carried. One of the black men was gathering sticks to make a fire; the other was on guard, but his eyes were distracted by a group of magpies on the opposite side of the river.

Murra signalled to Alinta to lie down. She did – without making a sound. Then she watched how Murra moved towards the clearing on the river bank and stepped forward from the shelter of the trees, spear ready. A surge of pride at the sight of him almost drowned her fears.

The strangers stared in shock. Some tried to grab their polished clubs, but their leader leapt to his feet and called out to them, so they stopped. They talked urgently to each other, until Murra spoke: 'You are in Nyari land! You have entered without permission! You are not welcome here!'

There was more urgent talking; then the leader spread out his arms as if he wanted to embrace everything, and he called out in his own strange tongue. One of the black men shouted something which Alinta did not understand, nor did Murra. It was obvious he came from a distant place. He then signalled in sign language that they had come in peace and had brought many gifts.

The leader gestured anxiously towards the other men who held up strange glittering things which sparkled in the light like clear water. They had necklaces made of brightly coloured stones, and many other things.

But Murra did not stay; he stepped back to where Alinta waited, and together they hurried back to tell the people what they had seen.

Turuga and the others were surprised to see the two return before their time was up, but when they heard the news they said they had done well to return. The men set out to find the intruders – to send them away before they could do any harm.

Towradgi's eyes were on Hair-of-Fire. She saw there was a great struggle in his mind – fear, excitement, indecision. Should he go along, or stay behind and hide? Turuga called out to him: he was needed to tell the strangers that they were not wanted here. So Hair-of-Fire went with them.

Alinta stayed with the women. A shadow had fallen over the joy at her impending marriage. She told the women of the canoe, and how the men who had moved it forward had their backs in the direction they were going so that they could not see where they were heading.

Later in the day they heard the noise of breaking twigs, and the sound of harsh voices, and of people crashing through the bush. The warriors were bringing the strangers back with them. The two strongest men were lugging between them a big, heavy chest which made their progress difficult.

Their leader walked with Hair-of-Fire. He was not tall but of sturdy build. His hair and beard were cut short, but sprouted like the wings of a flying bird on his upper lip. His face, like those of the others, was red, and rivulets of sweat ran down into his beard and down his neck. He did not look like a warrior.

Soon the strangers were seated by the fires, and they were given water mixed with honey, fish and fruit. They spoke noisily amongst themselves. Only the two black men kept apart, and they were ignored by the people because they must have known the Law, and they had brought these unwelcome visitors without permission.

The Nyari men looked at the gifts the strangers offered, and they handled them with much astonishment. They offered goods in barter for those things they fancied, but when the strangers wanted to press their gifts on them for nothing, they let them lie and turned away.

The women kept away and went about their business. Still, they were curious. Wonda finally caught Hair-of-Fire's eye and he came across, quite flustered, his mind preoccupied. He told her quickly what he had learnt, so that she could explain to the others. It seemed the leader's name was 'Goodman', and he had come because he had heard much about the Nyari people, their customs, their valour, and their land, and he had wanted to meet with them and honour them.

Alinta remembered how Hair-of-Fire had often told them stories about the people of his nation: how the elders there were pitiless and had great power over men like him. And how many who – like he – had been banished from their country had become cruel and violent, and were best avoided. It was obvious he was not afraid of Goodman and his companions, and soon he was sitting with them once again, explaining to them and the elders what both sides were saying.

The women looked at Towradgi, but her face was still, and she seemed to be lost in thought.

When the men had eaten, Goodman looked about, got to his feet, stretched himself, and walked to a place from where one could see the distant hills. Hair-of-Fire and the others followed.

'How much of this is Nyari land?' Goodman asked, and Hair-of-Fire flung his arm wide and told him it stretched as far as the eye could see, and further. And there was pride and love in his voice and in his eyes.

Goodman was impressed, and Turuga smiled when he saw his admiration. 'Yes,' Turuga said, 'this is the land of the Nyari. This is our heart and our spirit, the breath of our body. From the eternal it has been handed down to us; we are its keepers. We are the land, and the land is us.'

It seemed that Hair-of-Fire had some trouble explaining what Turuga meant, because he was asked many questions. He stared at his feet and listened, his lips pinched; then he scratched his head and spoke again. Goodman and the others exchanged looks and smiles amongst themselves which made Hair-of-Fire's face turn red as the blood rushed to his cheeks.

Turuga and the elders had watched patiently, but at last Turuga asked 'What did Goodman say?'

'Goodman would like to come and live here with his family and friends.' Hair-of-Fire shot a quick, sideways glance at Goodman, and there was a touch of malice as he said: 'He has a wife and seven daughters...' This caused some astonishment and pity: was there something wrong with him? Had he no sons? Hair-of-Fire spoke of the animals Goodman and his friends would bring. He mentioned not only those he had spoken of before, but also animals that looked like clouds before a rainy day, whose meat was good to eat, whose hair was warm... warmer than possum fur.

But Turuga and the elders did not want any more clay-face people to come into their land, and they told Hair-of-Fire to pass on these words, which he did. After this there was a ceremony in which Goodman asked Turuga and the elders to make a sign on what looked like a thin, pale piece of bark. Hair-of-Fire explained this was like a message stick and would be used to show the elders of Goodman's nation that he had been in Nyari land.

Goodman and his companions were told where they could make camp. When they had gone the people prepared for Alinta's wedding.

Murra and Alinta knelt before Turuga while the others stood around, and he tied the sacred string around their shoulders. They were painted with white and yellow and red ochre, and there was singing and dancing, as there had always been since the coming of the Ancestors.

But not far away was the campfire of Goodman and his companions, and whenever Alinta raised her eyes she could see it glowing in the dark.

Hair-of-Fire, too, looked across, tempted, restive, and at last he went to sit and talk with them. Towradgi had seen that he was troubled, that his own kind was calling him, and that he did not know what to do.

Next morning he had gone.

Goodman and his companions had left before dawn, and he had gone with them. The camp site was abandoned, and the only thing that was left was the smouldering ash of their fires.

Wonda cried and wailed and cut her skin with a sharp stone to help her bear her grief. She had grown fond of him; she had thought they would have a good life together. Alinta and the others sat with her and tried to comfort her. Some of the young men wanted to follow Goodman and bring Hair-of-Fire back, but Turuga and the elders did not think they should. They were grave, but not surprised: he wanted to return to his own people. Let him. He would be back. Had he not often said how much evil there was among his countrymen?

Towradgi, too, comforted her pupil. She thought of the visions she had had by the river a long time ago. She felt again the keen edge of a great sorrow, and she did not understand why it must happen to her people. All around her was the beauty of the morning; the kookaburras laughed and cackled, magpies sang their song, the air was fresh and clean. 'The Great Spirit's wisdom is deeper than that of man,' she murmured. 'He knows that good can come out of evil, and knowledge out of suffering . . .'

Hair-of-Fire was seated in the canoe with Goodman and the others. He was dressed like them now, and he thought of many things. Would he be pardoned, like Goodman had said, or would he once more be put in chains? He felt sick at the thought of it, and the terror of the past loomed up in front of him. Had he been a fool to listen to the promises Goodman had made?

Promises that some of the land he had grown to love would belong to him, and him alone. He looked at the trees along the riverbank, at the flowering wattle, bright golden-yellow, at the tall reeds as they floated past, and he thought of the beauty of the land, and how rich it was, how fertile. He who had once been a creature of contempt, a hireling without a penny to his name, flogged, treated like a dog, would be a man of stature and of wealth.

He glanced at his companions. It had been strange to hear them speak at first: words he had not heard for a long time echoed in his thoughts and brought back memories of home. He thought of his wife and child, and all those dear to him.

Then he thought of what he had now left behind. He thought of Wonda and her cheerfulness, of all the others who had become his brothers, sisters, father, mother. He remembered the freedom he had felt when he and the others walked through the bush with their spears, their woomeras. All this began to look like a dream. Tears came to his eyes, but he was anxious to hide them from the others who would never have understood that he had been happy with 'the savages'. It may well have been partly true what Goodman had suggested: that he had been ensnared by magic. He must return to his own kind. He looked at Goodman, and he knew only too well that many more like him would come. Like him, and worse. There could be bloodshed.

He had to show his countrymen that he was of great use to them. And he had to find a way to make the Nyari leave their land – or part of it – without battle.

When they made camp for the night, he explained his plan to Goodman who slapped him on the shoulder and was very pleased and appreciative.

The Nyari had set out on their journey back to the sea. The men led the way – on the lookout for kangaroo and emu, and on guard against danger. Suddenly they stopped, aghast, almost unable to believe their eyes. They called to the women to turn back, to take the children, to avert their eyes: for cut and branded into the bark of the biggest trees were their sacred, secret signs, symbols of power, symbols only those men were allowed to see who had passed their initiation. To defy that Law laid down by the Ancestors meant death.

They found the tracks of Hair-of-Fire and the others, and they saw that he had betrayed his clan, and had defied the Ancestors, using the knowledge they had given him. As long as those signs remained, no woman, child, or uninitiated youth could stay in or pass through this area. The place was now filled with destructive power, the harmony of life destroyed.

Years passed. Alinta had become one of Murra's clan. They noticed little of the strangers, because their land was far from the sea. But every time a visitor passed through, or when the tribes met at their large gatherings for barter, ceremonies, story-telling, there were more tales about the clay-face people. Tribes had been driven from their land by the weapons the strangers carried. It was known now that the weapons they had seen could, with a crack of thunder, hurl small things like stones over long distances, and they could kill. Murra had seen one of them: it had been taken from a man injured in a battle. It was small, round, and very heavy. Some tribes had been pushed into the land of neighbouring nations, causing hostility where there had long been peace.

It was said that the clay-face people built big mia-mias out of rocks, and in them were kept many of their own kind who, by all accounts, were miserable. They could be seen in groups, tied together, cutting pathways through the bush and hills. Some were dressed all the same, in something that was red like blood, and it was they who had the power. There were few women, fewer children. It was clear that the arrival of these strangers meant danger not only to the People, but to the very land itself.

It was the time of the festival of Pal-ly-an. Many women would come and meet at the sacred site, women from many places in Nyari land.

Alinta was coming too. She and Murra now had a son, Eaglehawk, and they came to show him to Kiah, Turuga, Towradgi, and the others.

Alinta found Towradgi seated on a log some distance from the camp. She was now very old. Her eyes had sunk deep, deep, into their sockets; her voice sounded as if it were coming from far away; her movements were slow. She was teaching two young girls, as she had done when Alinta and Wonda had been children. At first she did not see Alinta and her son, and so Alinta sat down and listened.

'. . . And when they had killed the Evil One,' Towradgi said, 'the elders told the warriors: "The body of the Evil One is dead, but his spirit is still alive. It will try to escape and take many forms. As soon as the fire is lit we must kill every living thing that crawls from it." And as the flames roared up a kangaroo jumped from them, and the warriors killed it. Then came an eaglehawk, a dingo, a goanna, a snake, a lizard, and many other beings. And when the fire had almost died, a caterpillar crawled from it. But a warrior stamped on it and threw it back.

'"At last," they said, "this is the end of the Evil One. No longer can he take the form of any animal."' Towradgi paused, and the children and Alinta waited.

'But they did not think of man. And it is in the form of man that the Evil One appears, and makes trouble everywhere . . .'

Alinta knew the story her old tutor told. Indeed, the Evil One was alive. There was a feeling of forthcoming destruction in the air; it seemed to hover just beyond the things that were visible, waiting to pounce, to devour everything in its path. Alinta held her son close to her, and she wondered how she could protect him from what was bound to happen.

When the women set out for the sacred site they came across strange tracks. Some of them were made by men like Goodman and his companions whose feet were encased in a second skin that obscured their toes. But there were others, heavier, that had churned up the earth and thrown about small pads of soil and grass.

The women were filled with fear, for this intrusion was a violation of this place. To let it pass would be to offend the Ancestors who had entrusted the site to them. They cautiously moved on. They could smell a fire burning, and they heard voices, and some snorting sounds. Then they saw three creatures, big and powerful. They were animals, but different from any they had ever seen: long hair was growing from their necks and buttocks; their legs were strong – like slender trees. But their muscles moved under their skin, suggesting great strength. They had been grazing, but now they stood, alert. Their ears, like those of kangaroos, pricked up and twitched this way and that as they listened.

Not far from them a mia-mia had been erected, and three men were there. Clay-face men.

They were busy skinning a kangaroo, and the hair of one of them burnt like fire in the sun. Wonda cried out as she saw who it was. He turned as he heard the sound and peered into the bush, and the others stopped what they were doing. They were smeared with blood.

Towradgi stood quite still, trembling with rage and pain at this sacrilege that had been committed and could not be undone. But it could be punished. Could be avenged. Old as she was, she rushed forward, her digging stick held high, and screamed. The others followed.

Those who were with Hair-of-Fire grabbed their thunder-sticks, but he yelled out to them and faced the women. He called Towradgi's name, and he called her 'Mother' as he used to do. He wanted to explain, but she did not listen. She was at the fire and pulled apart the burning embers.

Alinta and the others picked up the burning wood and threw it at the mia-mia the men had built. The animals reared up and tore free and ran away, and the men for a moment did not know what to do. They shouted at Hair-of-Fire, and he yelled back at them, and then he held onto Towradgi, and made her stop. Alinta and Wonda hurried to her assistance, but one of the men fired his thunderstick in the ground so that earth and stones flew up. The women froze, not sure what to do. Hair-of-Fire let go of Towradgi and stood back: he still had respect for her.

There was quiet for a moment, and they all caught their breath. Towradgi was the first to speak, and her voice was very low. She said: 'You! You have done this, Hair-of-Fire! We took you from the sea when you could have died of hunger and thirst. We shared everything with you. You put our sacred signs for everyone to see; you have come here when you know this place is sacred to the women. We taught you the secrets of life, and you have betrayed us!'

The other men stared at Towradgi and then asked questions of Hair-of-Fire, but he did not answer. Instead he spoke to Towradgi in a choking voice: 'This place is ours now; it was given to us by the elders of our own nation.'

And she said: 'It is not theirs to give.'

He forced himself to be firm and quiet, and he spoke to her as if she were a child: 'We shall build our mia-mias here, Mother, and we shall live here, and this place will be for our children, and our children's children and their children after that. And there is nothing you can do.'

Towradgi's face became like black stone, and her eyes were fierce and burnt with anger. She pulled herself to her full height, and pointed at him, and she said: 'I curse you, Hair-of-Fire, I curse you. May the earth swallow you. I curse you and these men. No goodness will be around you, no sun will shine on you. The being of darkness will follow you all your days to the edge of eternity. Even now he stands at your shoulder. Greed will not let you rest; you will find no peace in this land – you and your children, and your children's children.'

The women stood and shivered when they heard Towradgi; they could feel around them the great power Towradgi had. And Hair-of-Fire was afraid. So were the other men who had not understood a word.

Alinta saw a flash of lightning and heard the crack of thunder; she saw Towradgi stagger and fall, clutching her side. The women screamed with terror, and Hair-of-Fire, too, was horrified and turned on his companions. While he and they were shouting at each other, Alinta and Wonda helped Towradgi to her feet, and they half led, half carried her away with the others.

On the way back to their camp Towradgi died.

They laid her on a wooden frame covered with boughs and leaves and grass, and they gave her her staff, her coolamon, her dilly bag and wrapped her in her cape of possum fur. Then the women sat around her and gave way to their great grief. In the distance the curlew called – the curlew, the bird of death. It was an eerie, lonely call, like a woman crying. The men painted themselves with ochre, and they set out to revenge her death, and the desecration of the site.

Hair-of-Fire knew that he and his companions had transgressed against the Law. He knew the warriors would look for them, but he wondered if they would follow him into the area sacred to the women, or would lie in wait outside. He felt uneasy: the place was hostile now. The trees stood in silent reprehension; the birds did not sing. He had lived too long with the Nyari to shake off their teachings. He remembered

Towradgi's curse. Already something she had said was coming true: he could find no rest.

His companions scoffed, and he resented it. He felt offended by the way they talked about the women, especially the one who would have been his wife. When he showed his anger, they laughed and taunted him. Still, he insisted they get away, and so at last they left. They rode a long way, and then made camp.

Turuga and Murra and the others found their tracks where they had left the sacred area, and followed them. For three days and two nights they followed, and when they smelt their fire they waited until it was dark again.

The moon was full, and the trees stood black against the silver-blue translucent sky. Hair-of-Fire knew the sounds of the bush at night and he listened, every muscle tense, for something or someone coming. He could hear the bells of their grazing horses, the gurgling of the creek; he could hear the thumping sound the kangaroo makes when it hops away; and he heard the possums cough and squabble, and the rustle of dry twigs and leaves as the echidna looked for ants. He watched the shadows among the trees, and sometimes he thought he saw a man, and his hair stood on end and his mouth went dry.

Then he noticed he could no longer hear their horses, and he called his companions to look for them. Hair-of-Fire sat by himself and stared into the fire, and he could see Towradgi's face in the flames. He heard the curlew call; it was strange that the bird had come so far inland, and he knew that it cried for him.

He got to his feet because he could not bear to be alone, and he called the names of his companions, but there was no answer. He was seized by an overwhelming dread and, like a man who has lost his sight and mind, he ran in the direction they had taken. Further and further from the camp he went, calling their names, now thinking he could hear the horses snorting, or could hear a human voice.

At last he found his companions. They were lying in the bright light of the moon, flung back into the soft, young, grass; blood still ran from the wounds where the spears had pierced their bodies.

When he turned he saw the black edge of the bush, and the glow of his fire. Between him and it, out of the shadows, came those who once had been his friends, his brothers, their gleaming dark bodies painted with the signs of war, their spears ready.

So Hair-of-Fire died, and his body and those of his companions were left lying where they had fallen, and their animals ran free.

The elders decided that the people should move into the hills though it was early, well before the usual time. They would meet with other members of the nation, and they would unite and drive out the people with faces like pipe-clay.

Alinta and her people moved over the plain towards the mountains whose peaks were in the clouds, as they often were at this time of the year. A strong wind was blowing, and it did not stop for days. It would be cold up in the hills.

As Alinta looked around it seemed to her that the whole world was filled with desperate anger. The trees were swaying, shaking their branches against the ashen sky; the grass was lying flat; crows flew up now and then, their voices harsh, forboding. There was a strange timelessness about this scene, and it seemed to Alinta as if she saw something she would see again a long long time hence.

They set up camp by the river. The men built windbreaks, and temporary mia-mias were constructed. Here they were protected, and it was peaceful, while above them the wind was still roaring as he shook the crowns of the eucalypts. The people were subdued. They spoke quietly of what had happened, of what was to be done.

Alinta had rocked her son to sleep. She looked at Murra who was sitting opposite, staring into the remnants of a small fire they had lit. She remembered how – and it seemed long ago – she had seen him standing on a dune, waiting to come into the camp; how he had put around her neck the string of eucalyptus seeds which she was still wearing, how they had walked together through the bush and seen the wombat on their first day of self-discipline. Her heart ached with love for him. He was a good man. He was kind and gentle, powerful and brave, and to be trusted.

He looked up, and a faint smile creased his face. He loved her and their child; he was proud of them. 'Soon we shall go to my people,' he said softly, 'There are no strangers there . . .'

Suddenly the guards came running, shouting; it was as if the earth was trembling, and as the people looked towards the open plain they saw something coming at great speed. Out of the night they came, the clay-faced ones, on their animals. The rumbling sound grew like thunder as hard feet pounded the earth.

The men grabbed their spears, their woomeras; the women took the children, still drowsy, half asleep. The blast of thunder-sticks cracked the night; there were screams of terror, there was yelling, shouting; there was fire as the mia-mias began to burn; there were the cries and wails of children.

Alinta saw her mother's face, briefly lit by the flames; she saw Warroo falling, hands pressed against her head and red with blood; she saw the camp dogs running, tails between their legs; she saw the men with faces of pipe-clay towering above, heard their animals calling in high frightened voices, their eyes rolling, as they were forced to trample everything before them.

Then she saw Murra falling. She ran to him, their child in her arms, and she saw that he was dying, and she could barely understand what he said. He wanted her to hide by the river, and so she dodged spears and bullets, and ducked, and crawled to where the reeds were high. There she stood in the water, clutching her son to her who whimpered, terrified. But the strangers did not hear because they shouted and yelled to each other, and after a while that was the only thing that could be heard, because the people were all dead.

At last there was nothing but the crackling of the fire, and the sound of the wind in the trees above. The men with faces of pipe-clay had gone.

For a long time Alinta did not move. When at last she did, the wind had stopped; her child lay asleep against her breast.

Slowly she came from the water, and she saw the devastation in the first light of dawn. Smoke had filled the air with a strange haze, and she walked through it among the ashes and the dead. There was her father, there her mother. There was Morrorra, clutching his spear; there was Warroo, and Wonda, and all the others she had loved; there were the children, the two girls Towradgi had told the story of the Evil One. They all lay there, many with open, unseeing eyes, already glazed, their bodies sprawling, rigid in death.

There was Murra. She sat down next to him and gently touched his face. And she wished she and her child were dead, dead with all the others.

So she sat, and the sun came through the haze and tinted everything brownish-red. Kookaburras began to cackle somewhere in the bush. Alinta cut herself with sharp stones to help her bear her grief, and then she began to chant the words she had learnt from Towradgi and the other women, honouring the dead and sending their spirits safely to their home.

When all this was done, she took her child, and she began on the long journey to Murra's people.

M a y d i n a,
the Shadow

W hen Maydina realized the time had come, she and Takari, a woman of the Bunnerong tribe, quietly, furtively, went away to a secluded spot among the tea-tree. There, on the clean sand, to the sound of the surf pounding the shore, she gave birth to a daughter.

She had planned to kill the child the moment it was born, but when Takari handed her the baby, and she saw the small body, the tiny clutching hands, when she heard the cry of a new being just born into a hostile world, she could not do it. What did it matter now that a whitefeller was the father? Her daughter was her flesh, her blood, her body. This child would live. She held her close, and she felt a great surge of love; it was the first good feeling she had had for many years.

Takari understood, and so the two women slowly made their way back towards the old shack between the dunes and rocks – Maydina carrying the child, Takari supporting her as best she could.

They were forced to live here on this wild and rugged shore with two sealers; Alf and Joe. Their true husbands were dead: Maydina's had been shot by Alf when he was in a drunken rage;

Takari's had been killed by squatters who had caught him spearing a sheep.

It was evening, and the sun was close to setting, so that the rocks and cliffs stood out black against the gold and purple of the sea.

Back in the hut the fire had gone out and Takari hastily pushed some wood together to attend to it. Maydina had a few moments rest, the baby wrapped in a piece of blanket in her arms. She was full of fear: now that she had decided that the child would live she thought that Alf might kill it. She wondered if she should have run away. But she would not have got very far: she was exhausted and it would be easy for Alf to catch up with her and murder both of them.

Many times she and Takari had talked about escape, but had not dared to take the actual step. Their own lands were far away; they were now living in the land of another nation and were here without permission of those who had looked after it according to the Law. The spirits would be angry and might punish them if they walked through the bush. And even if the spirits understood their plight, there were white men who would capture them – men just as bad as, perhaps worse than, Alf and Joe.

At last they heard heavy footsteps and voices, gruff and loud. Takari and Maydina looked at one another: Maydina was resolved that she would fight for her daughter's life.

The men stooped to enter, and for a moment they blocked out the light as they came through the narrow door. They moved about, their presence filling the small shack as they hung up a fishing net, threw down some tools, their guns. The women waited, every muscle tense.

Joe was the first to see the child. He stopped, his small eyes staring under bushy brows. He said something to his mate, and Alf slowly came across. The two looked down at Maydina and her child, and for a few moments time stood still. Maydina felt her heart pounding against her ribs, felt the baby close to her, as if she and it were still one creature.

Joe sniggered suddenly, turned, and got a bottle from the shelf. Alf continued to stare. His face was in shadow; Maydina did not know what he thought or planned.

'A boy?' he asked at last.

'No,' Maydina forced herself to say.

Takari had lit a lamp, and it was now swinging from the rafter, casting a restless light on those below. The baby whimpered and turned to find Maydina's breast. Alf watched as it began to suck. Something stirred in him: a faint realization that here was a new being, one that was part of him. He knew he had power over these two lives, and he thought that it was as it had to be. They were his; he could do what he liked with them. A daughter! He wished it had been a son. Though, coming to think of it, it mattered little. Many of these children died . . . so might this one. The blacks were weak.

He sat down with Joe and took the bottle that was offered. When he had drunk he wiped his mouth with his sleeve and looked at Maydina and the child once more.

'You make sure she's quiet, do you hear me, woman? Don't want no whimpering bastards here . . .' That was all he said.

Tears of relief came to Maydina's eyes.

She called her daughter Biri – 'flowering wattle'.

She worked hard; harder than before which had been hard enough. She was afraid to cause any anger because in a fit of temper Alf might bash the baby. She helped skinning seals; she fetched and carried, chopped wood, did everything that was asked of her; she lay with him at night though she hated the stench that came from him, hated his hard cruel hands, hated every fibre of his body. She hated his mind, his spirit.

So life continued. Days turned into nights, seasons into years. The men went about their business slaughtering seals and pulling off their skins. When they had sufficient, another man would come with his horse and cart, and they'd all take the skins away. And then there would be peace.

With Alf and Joe away, Maydina and Takari breathed more freely. But for these spells their spirits would have died. Then they talked about their own lands, and dreamt of ways of getting there unharmed. They talked of the days when they had been children and were still with their clans.

White men had been about, and the children had been warned to keep away from them. The old people often told of the times before their coming and how free they had been to roam the land. Now when they moved from place to place, they found their way barred by fences here and there, their waterholes often soiled and muddied by herds of alien animals. There were stories of massacres, of whole clans dying after eating white man's food which had a bitter taste. Still, the childhood days seemed beautiful to the two women. Maydina remembered swimming with the other children in the river, sitting around the fires, listening to stories; she remembered the closeness of the people, the love she felt for those around her, and their love for her.

When Biri was old enough to talk, Maydina taught her the language of her people, told her which among the animals and plants were her friends, taught her songs and stories she herself had learnt. She could still respond to the many moods of the sea and the land; was still touched by the beauty of the gently heaving water on a calm, moonlit night; still felt her spirits rise at the sight of an eagle soaring in the sky, still loved to watch as the wind played in the grass behind the dunes.

Often she wondered when the Great Spirit would punish those who had transgressed against the Law of the Ancestors. Sometimes, when a great gale blew and sent the breakers crashing against the shore so that crests of foam seemed to reach the very clouds, when endless torrents of rain fell from a dark, threatening sky, then she thought the time had come, and she and Takari were filled not only with fear, but a fierce wish that it be so. They wanted to see the invaders punished, wanted to see them driven from the land, sucked back into the sea from where they had come. But the skies cleared, the storms subsided, and Maydina would hold Biri in her arms, glad that the child was safe. One day the time would come; this she knew. Perhaps by then both she and Biri would be dead.

Biri was Maydina's second child. She remembered with anguish her first-born, a son by her true husband. The boy had been affected by some evil magic that had come with the invaders: it made children as well as adults waste away and cough up blood. She had seen others die of it, too. Her spirit rose in fierce determination to protect her daughter.

Biri had grown and was old enough to help the women with their chores. Despite the rags she wore – remnants of an old flour bag – she was beautiful: her eyes were large and clear and very dark; her skin a golden brown, her body lean and agile. Maydina was proud of her, and at the same time was consumed by a constant worry as to how she could guard her from the white men, who often forced young girls, even children, to their will. She had seen it happen. She did not trust Alf, even though he was her father. Nor did she trust his mate, who was getting tired of Takari – Takari, who was growing thin and was coughing blood like Maydina's child had done. She was relieved that the two men seemed to take no notice of young Biri, even if when they spoke to her they spoke in curt commands, as some speak to their dogs.

One day they were all on the beach, unloading the skins of seals. It was winter, and the sea was grey, like lead; the wind bit through the rags they wore. Biri had looked for shelter behind some rocks and stood there shivering.

It was then that Maydina heard Alf tell his mate that he would hand over Biri to another sealer; she was big enough now to be useful to the man. Maydina's heart seemed to stop, but then the blood rushed through her body, and there was a roaring in her head.

She could hear herself cry out, 'You not give my daughter to this man!'

Alf looked at her. 'Who's to stop me? You?' he said, and told her to get the fire started in the hut.

Maydina, Biri and Takari made their way back to the shack, laden with skins, fishing nets and knives, and driftwood for the fire. But Maydina did not feel the load she carried, the rocks under her feet, the cold wind on her skin. She only had one thought: to escape. The time had come. She told Takari. Takari nodded. They looked back: Alf was still at the boat, Joe was following them.

They must gain time.

They turned around one of the large rocks, Maydina grabbed a large chunk of wood, and they waited. When Joe passed she brought it down on his head with all the strength she had. He fell and lay still.

The women ran, dragging Biri along with them. Soon Takari began to lag behind, seized by a fit of coughing. Maydina called out to her, but ran on with her daughter. Behind them was the roaring of the sea as the breakers hit the shore. Then there was a shot; Maydina turned and saw Takari fall, and she saw Alf come running from the boat, brandishing the gun he always had with him.

She rushed back to help Takari, but she saw her friend's eyes fixed in the stare of death. She hurried back to Biri and dragged her away with her, while the wind tore at the rags she wore and blew her sideways against the rocks. They struggled on till they reached some scrub. Through this they crawled, not caring, not even noticing, how the hard branches cut their skin. Then they lay flat and still, and through an opening they saw Alf running past, yelling their names, ordering them to stop and to come to him. They could see him hesitate, turn, look around, but they had left no prints on the rocks and stones that a white man could have seen, and it was getting dark.

When night had come, they slowly crept from their hiding place. Biri asked about Takari, and Maydina whispered that she must not say the name of one who died, and that she had gone to her spirit home. Maydina had decided that there was no other way but to brave the dangers of this unknown land, and to make for the country where she herself was born, that her people had held in trust since the time of the Ancestors. It was called Billagal.

She knew they had to travel towards the setting sun, and so they spent many days moving in that direction. Often they had to abandon the path they followed for fear of meeting men, and then they would scramble through dense bush. At night they would sleep, huddled against each other, in a hollow log or cave, or underneath the shelter of some shrubs. They found food, but Maydina did not want to make a fire for fear of being noticed and so they were often cold.

They would come across signs that the white men had been here: they found the desolate stumps of large trees, their branches and twigs and leaves scattered not far away. Maydina knew that spirits had lived in many of these trees, and wondered where they were. They came across fences, and the animals of the white man stood grazing where once there had been wallabies and kangaroos. Tracks had been cut through the bush, and now and then they heard the sound of creaking wheels. They would hide in the grass and shrubs, and see the bullockies go past, wielding their long whips, or men on horses.

Once they saw a group of them, in uniforms, taking along with them six men of the people. They were fixed to the horses with chains around their necks and wrists, and there was a look of hopelessness on their faces. Maydina stared at them, and her heart was sore: she wondered where they were heading, what their fate would be, and there was nothing she could do to help.

One morning Maydina and Biri came across a camp site in the bush. A tent had been erected, a fire was burning brightly; close by a horse and donkey rested. No human being was in sight, but then Maydina heard a man's voice raised in some kind of singing. It came from the direction of the creek, together with the sound of splashing water.

Maydina gestured to Biri to lie down; then, after a moment's hesitation, she hurried to the tent. Here she might find something to keep Biri warm during the cold nights.

The animals watched, ears pricked; the voice continued singing its tuneless little song. Maydina peered into the tent: there was no one inside, but on the ground there was a blanket. And there was some meat, already cooked. She snatched up the blanket, took the meat, and was slipping from the tent when a hand descended on her arm.

She whirled around and looked into the eyes of a man. He was quite old; he had a bushy beard, already grey, and grey hair came out from underneath his hat, so that one could see little of his face which was tanned and wrinkled.

Maydina, quick as lightning, snatched up a tomahawk that was lying there. She stood, ready to defend herself. The man stepped back, startled. Then he talked as one would talk to a wild animal: 'Easy now,' he said, 'easy . . .' He stood, hands raised, palms pointing towards her, to show he meant no harm.

Maydina shot a quick anxious glance to where she had left Biri, and he realized that someone else was there. It worried him, and he spoke loudly so that whoever it was could hear: 'I want no trouble; I'm a poor man, I got no money, got no gold . . .' He had no teeth, and it was hard to understand what he said.

Maydina understood that he, too, was afraid. He did not seem a violent man. She muttered that all she wanted was some food, a blanket.

The man, one eye still on the bush where the unseen presence hovered, exclaimed that she should have asked; he'd have given it to her. He was now anxious to show his friendliness; he told her he liked her people, that for many years he'd had one of her kind live with him, a woman called Timmallee, and that she had died not long ago. As he spoke his eyes grew moist, and his voice shook a little. Maydina was surprised that a white man could shed tears. Slowly her fear subsided, and when he asked her to sit down by the fire, she decided to call Biri from her hiding place.

The man's name was Mueller, and when he saw Biri emerge – shyly, hesitantly – from the bush, he could not stop chuckling to himself, partly from relief that there was no danger, partly at his own unnecessary fear, partly because he was pleased to have company.

Soon they were all seated and Mueller, brewing tea and feeding his guests with meat and damper, told them he came from a different land – not the one that had been the home of most of the white men. He did not think much of them, and he pulled faces to show his disgust at what they did. Biri watched him, wide-eyed and amazed, and slowly, gradually, she'd laugh at his ways which, in turn, encouraged him to continue with his stories. He pointed at some tools and explained he was a fossicker, and that he looked for gold. Maydina and Biri did not know what he meant. He scratched his head, wondering how to explain, and then, with a sudden impulse to confide in his visitors, he pulled out a small leather bag from underneath his shirt. After a furtive look around, his gnarled fingers dived into it and – as if divulging a great secret – produced a few oddly shaped yellow stones.

Maydina looked, but did not try to touch them. It seemed to her that he thought they were imbued with a great power.

Then, having put the stones away, he asked Maydina what she planned to do. Maydina haltingly told him that they were on their way to her own country – Billagal. He knew the place, knew it was fine country. He had been there not long ago. Then he shook his head. 'No blackfellers there now, Maydina. They all gone. Sheep country now. Sheep and cattle . . .'

Maydina sat in silence, filled with overwhelming grief. Deep in her heart she had known, and now it had been confirmed in words. She looked into the fire, and in her mind's eye she saw the land of Billagal, its plains and hills and rivers. She saw it as she had seen it when she was a child. She could feel the suffering of the land as if it was part of her own body.

Biri and Maydina stayed with Mueller the whole day. It was good for Biri to have a rest, for Maydina to have time to think.

Night came. Biri was asleep. Maydina was lost in silence. Mueller, too, was quiet. There was no other sound except the crackling of the flames, of the wind touching the leaves of the eucalypts. At last Mueller spoke. 'You stay with me,' he said. 'I'll look after you . . . you and your daughter.' He was a lonely man; the woman and the child would give some meaning to his life again. He waited, hopefully, certain that Maydina would accept the offer.

Maydina raised her eyes: he was kind, meant well. But he was old. He would not be strong enough to defend her and her daughter against others. Yet what else could she do? Where could she go? Mueller took a flask from his pocket, uncorked it, licked his lips. Maydina felt a tinge of alarm. He caught her eye and thrust the bottle towards her. 'Here, have a sip,' he said, 'make you feel warm . . .' She shook her head. She could smell the rum, and it brought back memories of Alf. Now Mueller himself took a swig, sighed with content, then leaned forward to touch her thigh, reaching out for the warmth of another human being.

Maydina recoiled as if she had been hit, and she leapt to her feet. She knew only too well what drink could do. Not only had she seen Alf and Joe go mad with it – no longer in control of their bodies, their speech slurred, their minds confused, but she had seen others weep and laugh, and clamouring for a fight. She had seen them sick and vomiting. And she had seen what it could do to her own people. Once, before she had been brought to this area, she had caught sight of some of them staggering stupidly around or lying unconscious in the dirt – to the scorn of the white men who had made them drunk. Whatever Mueller said, she did not listen. She wanted to get away at once. Biri had woken up, but she was still drowsy. While Maydina was helping her to get to her feet, Mueller protested anxiously that he had meant no harm. To show his sincerity he put the bottle out of sight, behind a stack of wood.

At last Maydina calmed herself a little. Mueller, anxious to reassure her, offered that she and Biri should sleep in his tent while he would remain outside. This he promised. In the morning they would work out what to do.

Not far from Mueller's camp – within a day's travelling – there was a place called Balambool. There, Mueller told Maydina as he boiled the billy, she and her daughter would be safe. He would take them there. He told her that in that place there lived a woman who was very kind. She was a widow. Her husband had died falling off his horse, and she and her son were now in charge of what he called a Christian Mission. She took in many people who were without a home; she specially cared for women and young girls. There were no white men at Balambool, except her son – and he was known to be kind to her people.

Around the camp birds sang their morning song, dew sparkled and glittered on the grass and leaves. The sun peered through the branches and promised a fine day.

Maydina did not notice. She thought of Takari, and she envied her: Takari was at peace in her spirit home. But she, Maydina, was like a fugitive in a world that had lost its meaning. She was like a twig that had been blown into a dark, threatening sea, wrenched from a tree that itself seemed to wither and to die from the impact of a devastating storm. She looked at Biri, and saw that her child was watching her, her bright eyes shadowed with apprehension, wondering why her mother was so grave, so sad. Maydina turned to Mueller. Yes, they would go to Balambool.

When they arrived, the place seemed quite deserted. Mueller left Maydina and her daughter and went in search of someone he could tell that they had come. The only sign that people were about somewhere was a buggy in the yard, and a horse in the stable, munching hay and looking out.

Maydina shyly, fearfully, let her eyes wander over the sheds and buildings. She had seen places like this before – from a distance. She knew the people who lived in them were in charge of the many animals they had brought from their own country. She knew it was dangerous to be seen near these creatures with their thick, curly fur and plaintive voices. Whole clans had been massacred for killing and eating some of them.

There was a sadness about Balambool. Outside the main building, which had received a battering from the weather like all the other structures, there was a flower bush growing: pink, with thorns. At one side there were some trees Maydina had never seen before. Except one: it bore large red-green fruit which was good to eat.

Mueller returned. He helped Biri from the horse and then led her and Maydina along a path towards a grassy hill and a patch of trees. As they turned around a bend they found two groups of people standing there, assembled around a hole in the ground. Maydina realized it was an open grave, and this was a place where the dead were buried.

Mueller took off his hat, ran his fingers through his hair, and sat down to wait. Maydina remained on her feet, her eyes on those before her. The larger group was of the people. There were women, children, men; the latter were mainly elderly, and there were few. Some of them were painted with signs of mourning, according to the custom. One of the old men stood, leaning on a shovel. Next to him was a small boy. His head was bent so low she could not see his face, but his small figure showed the grief he felt. Perhaps it was a brother or a sister they were about to bury. Maydina drew her daughter close to her.

The smaller group of whites stood opposite: a woman and two men. The woman and one of the men were dressed in black, and the gusts of wind would now and then make their garments flutter so that they looked like huge crows preparing to fly up into the sky. The other man was younger, and he looked tall and strong.

The man in black was talking. His eyes were shut, his hands were folded, his lips were moving rapidly – it seemed almost as if he were afraid. Maydina could not hear what he said. The air was filled with the mournful cries of the currawongs which strutted among the graves, all of which bore white crosses.

Maydina watched the woman. She was different from any she had seen so far. Her face was plain but delicate and pleasant. Contrary to the others there who were filled with grief, many of them crying openly, she seemed elated as if something beautiful had happened. Mostly her eyes were closed, but when she opened them she seemed to look at something far away up in the sky, behind the clouds.

The coffin had been lowered, and the man in black threw some earth into the grave. 'Earth to earth, ashes to ashes, dust to dust …' More earth followed. '… In sure and certain hope of the resurrection to eternal life through Jesus Christ, our Lord …'

The old man near the grave furtively passed to the boy a small carved wooden turtle. It had been the dead child's totem.

'They shall hunger no more, neither thirst any more … neither shall the sun light on them, nor any heat …'

The boy, making sure the man in black was not looking, dropped the turtle into the open grave. It hit the coffin with a small thud.

Maydina had watched all this with growing consternation. It was a bad omen to arrive at a time of burial. On the other hand she was comforted by the sight of so many of her own kind. She wondered how – if she stayed – she would be received by them. Some, she could see, belonged to different nations.

The funeral was over, and the old man stayed behind to fill in the grave while every one else dispersed. The white woman, accompanied by the men of her colour, came towards Mueller and his charges. She listened briefly to his explanation regarding Maydina's and her daughter's plight, then said briskly, 'Come with me', and led the way back towards the house.

Here they were made to sit in the livingroom. It was a plainly furnished room, very clean. The only decoration was a portrait of a white man with long beard and bushy brows who looked down on them with a grave but benign expression. While they waited, Mueller told Maydina in a whisper that the woman's name was

58

'Mrs McPhee'. He told her to repeat it after him for it was important she remembered: it would please the lady. Maydina found it hard – like others of her people she was not used to forming the sound Mueller made between his teeth and lower lip. So she called her 'Mrs Bee'.

Soon Mrs McPhee entered with the man in black, whom she called 'Reverend Bligh'. She had in her hands a ledger in which she used to note who arrived at Balambool, and who left, or died. There were many who had dates with black crosses next to them. She had changed her black hat for a bonnet which covered all her hair and gave her face with its thin brows and pale lashes an austere look. Her eyes were very blue.

'What is your name, good woman?'

Maydina did not answer. She held her head low, but her eyes took in much of her surroundings. She was worried by the presence of the Reverend Bligh who stood next to Mrs McPhee, hands behind his back, chin jutting out, his black, piercing eyes fixed on her and on her child.

'Does she speak English?' Mrs McPhee turned to Mueller.

'Yes, she does.'

'That's good. We all speak English here. I won't have them talk in their native tongues . . .'

'Her name's Maydina.'

'. . . Maydina? We shall give her a good Christian one. We shall call her May.' Maydina felt uneasy. Why would they take her name? She was Maydina, named so by her people. Why must she give up her name?

Mrs McPhee wrote in her book, and for a few moments there were no other sounds but the scratching of the pen, and in the distance the bleating of the sheep, all shorn and bare in the cold winter wind.

As Mrs McPhee dipped her pen into the ink, she looked at Biri, who tried to hide behind her mother.

'And the child's name?'

'That's little Biri.'

Mrs McPhee smiled unexpectedly: she liked children, and for a moment one could see that she once must have been pretty, even beautiful. Biri looked back at her, round-eyed and serious.

'We'll call you Emily.' She wrote *Emily Brown* into her book. She had noticed that Biri's skin was lighter than her mother's.

'Her father was a white man, wasn't he?'

Mueller nodded.

Mrs McPhee was pleased. 'That's good. It's easier to train those who have white blood in them.'

She had turned to Mr Bligh with this information: he had not been in the country long, and she felt he needed guidance and advice. He grunted. He had not expected otherwise.

'Does the father know they have come here?'

Mueller shook his head. 'I don't think so; they ran away from him, and he lives a fair way from here . . .'

Mrs McPhee was relieved. Now and then there had been violent scenes when men had come to reclaim their women who had been granted refuge here. Vile language had been used; shots had been fired; one of the sheds had been set alight by a jackaroo from one of the neighbouring stations. Sheep had been let out to stray all over the countryside, and her son's favourite horse had been shot.

It was not only these ruffians who hated what was being done at Balambool; the squatters of the district were also hostile, filled with resentment, envy. Labour was scarce and they had trouble finding men able and willing to clear the land and tend their stock. Balambool employed blacks for nothing more than rations largely distributed by the government. They sanctimoniously complained that Mrs McPhee used slave labour on her property, and made submissions to the government that this kind of thing be stopped.

Mrs McPhee had taught herself to look on these tribulations as God's way of testing her. The more hardship she overcame in His name, the more certainty there was of a sweet after-life with Him. She was convinced that it had been His specific plan that she and her husband come to this land – to civilize and christianize the natives, so that their souls, too, might be granted entry into heaven.

She turned to Maydina and the child. 'Thanks be to the Lord,' she said, 'who has brought you here.' She closed the book, got up, and stretched out her hand to take Biri with her. 'Come with me, Emily,' she said.

Maydina leapt to her feet and put her arms around her daughter. 'Don't touch,' she said. 'She my daughter. She with me!'

Mrs McPhee quickly drew back her hand, startled by Maydina's manner. Mr Bligh was taken aback as well; it confirmed an impression he had already formed: the natives were unpredictable.

Mrs McPhee spoke slowly, as one would speak to a child: 'I'll not harm her, May. I'll give her a pretty frock, she'll eat with me and my son – and young Johnny – and she'll sleep on the back verandah . . .'

But Maydina did not listen. She shook her head. 'She with me, she my daughter.'

Mrs McPhee decided it was better to have patience. 'Very well,' she said pleasantly, 'but you'll learn what's best for her . . .'

Maydina and Biri said goodbye to Mueller. 'Cheer up,' he said to Biri, 'soon you'll be a lady.' Then he turned to Maydina and gave her a crooked grin. 'There are worse in this world than bible bashers . . .'

She did not know what he meant, but when she saw him ride away, she felt sad. She had farewelled a friend.

Mrs McPhee led Maydina and her daughter down a passage, her long skirt swishing as she walked. In a room which received little light through a small window but was warm and cosy from the light of a big fire in a hearth, they saw a woman cooking. She was elderly and dark and plump, and she wore a white cloth over her greying hair, and another over her grey frock. She stopped what she was doing, her eyes on the new arrivals.

'Maggie, this is the woman May and her daughter Emily,' Mrs McPhee said briskly. 'I'll leave them in your care.' And she departed.

The moment Mrs McPhee was out of earshot, a huge smile crinkled up Maggie's face, and then she asked – in the language – 'What is your country?'

How good it was to hear that sound! 'Billagal', Maydina answered.

Maggie nodded. 'I know these people . . .'

'They have all gone . . .' Maydina's voice was low.

For a moment they did not speak, their thoughts with those who had died. Then Maggie murmured softly: 'We are like seeds of grass, blown by the wind . . . A long time from now we'll come again, like grass comes from the seed.'

Great comfort and reassurance flowed from Maggie. Maydina looked at her: it was so soothing to hear those words.

Maggie had been baking bread. Now she broke a piece from a loaf. 'What is your sign?' she asked.

'Pund-jel, sign of the sun.'

Maggie's was the same. She said, 'My totem is the parrot.'

'Mine the Blue Crane.'

Maggie took Maydina in her arms and rocked her gently to and fro as if she were a child. They looked at one another: they were mother and daughter. Then Maggie stooped and hugged Biri. Finally she gave them each a piece of bread. 'Eat', she said, 'you're welcome.'

Maydina and Biri slowly chewed the bread, and for the first time Maydina felt a sense of peace.

The days were short, and it was dark by the time Maydina and Biri had been shown into a small stone hut not far from the house. It once had been a store room. Here they were to sleep for the time being; later a shelter would be built for them in the area the late Mr McPhee had set aside for his charges. They had each had a bath in a large wooden tub in the wash house, and they had been given fresh sack-like garments and two pairs of something Maggie explained with a chuckle were called 'bloomers'. They had eaten bread and meat, and drunk hot tea.

The silence of the evening was shattered by a loud clanging noise. Johnny, the small boy whose friend had been buried that afternoon, was hitting a metal plate with an iron rod: it was time for 'prayers', Maydina was told.

Soon Maydina could see figures drifting out of the dark into the glow of a lamp suspended from a beam in the bough shed. Maggie took Maydina and Biri with her, and they sat on one of the benches with the others under the leafy roof constructed of twigs and branches. It was a good feeling to be among those of her own kind. They looked at her curiously, kindly, accepting her as one of them.

The sides of the shed were open, and when the congregation had assembled, Maydina saw a small procession advancing from the house: Mrs McPhee, followed by old Tom and old Tim who carried between them a pedal organ. In the rear was little Johnny and the young man Maydina had seen at the funeral. 'That's Mister Edward, the Mistress's son,' Maggie whispered. 'He good fellow . . . I seen him born.' Maggie had been at Balambool for a long, long time.

Maydina watched him surreptitiously as he helped his mother to her place behind the organ. He was in his early twenties, well-built, and had an open, friendly face. She noticed that he gave a quick smile to one of the young women, and that she smiled back at him.

Soon voices and music rose from the bough shed while a light rain began to fall.

Once the song was finished, Mrs McPhee got to her feet and said: 'Let us pray.' She closed her eyes, after a long piercing look at Maydina, for it was important that she understood the significance of the occasion. Then, while everyone's head was lowered, Mrs McPhee spoke in a loud, imploring, voice: 'Oh Lord, in thy gracious wisdom thou hast brought into our midst yet two more souls so that they may be rescued from everlasting hell . . . forgive the woman May and her daughter Emily their past sinful lives, open their hearts and minds, so that they will let thee enter in thy glory and thy wisdom. Amen.'

Later that night Maydina lay on her wooden bunk, with Biri in her arm. Outside the rain was still coming down, but in the hut it was warm and dry. Maydina had not understood what Mrs McPhee had said in the bough shed; she had used words Maydina had never heard before: 'rescued', 'everlasting', 'glory', 'wisdom' . . . She had been puzzled that Mrs McPhee had locked the door of the hut so that she could not go out. Still, as she lay there with Biri next to her, she thought that it was good that they had come here.

Early next morning, as a strip of grey appeared in the east beneath the dark clouds, she heard the key turn in the lock. Not much later she and Biri were assembled once more in the bough shed with the others, singing 'hymns', which Maggie told her were in praise of the Great Spirit.

The winds had become warm; bright yellow wattles lit the countryside, followed by the lilac and purple of sarsaparilla and of the balmy mint bush in the hills. Delicate spider orchids began to venture forth in spots untouched by grazing. A blue crane built his nest by the waterhole near the house, and every morning and evening his strange voice would call out to Maydina, greeting her. He was her friend, her totem. It was a good sign that he had come.

The people at Balambool looked longingly across the plains and hills. It was the time of year when in the past they would have travelled far across the land, singing songs to the Ancestors, and meeting other tribes for barter and for ceremonies. Some left secretly, unable to resist; most of them stayed behind and merely sent their thoughts to where they could not go.

There was much work to be done at Balambool at this time of the year. The stocks increased, and there was need for more pasture. Paddocks had to be cleared and fenced; trees were ring-barked and grubbed, suckers cut: the bush was forever trying to reclaim the land.

Maydina worked long hours in return for rations; she helped with the ewes and their new-born lambs; she helped in the house. She learnt to clean and polish, cook and sew – though it was hard for hands that had been skinning seals to hold a needle. She began to understand that Mrs McPhee believed that constant labour pleased the Great Spirit and his son whose image was nailed to a cross in the bough shed. She learnt that his name was Jesus, that he was seated on a golden chair in a place called Heaven, waiting for all those who suffered. She went to the prayer meetings like the others, twice a day, and she began to enjoy the communal singing. She did not see much of Biri in the day; Mrs McPhee looked after her and the boy called Johnny. She taught the children to read and write, and she told them stories from a book she called the Bible and which she handled with great reverence. She also made them do small chores, such as weeding, dusting, sweeping.

Still, at night, after prayer, Maydina and Biri could be together. Then Maydina would teach Biri secretly, in the language, things she herself had been taught as a child. She told her of Baiame, the Great Spirit, who made the sun bring light to the dark earth. She told her how the Ancestors had walked over the bare plains and had created many things in his name, and had laid down the Law. She told her of the days the old people had described to her, days before the white man's coming, when they had been free to travel the land.

Once, during her first days at Balambool, she had sung a song to Biri, a song her mother used to sing. Mrs McPhee came into the hut, upset, angry. Had she not forbidden May to speak in the language? She must forget the old ways, the old life. It had been sinful.

She held up two pictures she had brought: one showed Jesus surrounded by blue-eyed angels with golden curls, seated among white clouds on a golden throne. The other showed a mob of black, red-tongued devils jumping around a fire, holding pitchforks, menacing a poor creature being roasted.

'Look,' Mrs McPhee had cried, 'look how evil! See the pitchforks? See the poor sinner being roasted over the flames of everlasting hell?' Then she had raised the other picture, and her voice had grown sweet and gentle: 'But this one . . . see how he lives in heaven, where there is peace and joy. Where will you go when you die?'

Maydina had not answered, but Biri had pointed quickly at the second picture, and Mrs McPhee had been very pleased.

Maydina received much help and guidance from old Maggie, Maggie who had come to Balambool when Mr McPhee was still alive, before Edward had been born. It seemed Mr McPhee had been much stricter than his wife. 'Too much kneeling' – Maggie chuckled and pulled a face – 'kneeling all the time. Knees hurting from too much kneeling . . .'

One day Maggie and Maydina were in the wash house. Clouds of steam surrounded them as they toiled. In the yard outside a man was saddling his horse. He was tall, sinewy, very dark. Like Edward he wore breeches, shirt, a wide-brimmed hat, but his feet were bare. He was Charlie, head stockman at Balambool. His real name was Joala. The boy Johnny was his son.

Maydina watched him through the open door, her work forgotten.

Maggie smiled. Then she said quietly: 'That Joala, you know, he looking for a wife ...'

Maydina hastily resumed her work. Then she said in a low voice, so low, one almost couldn't hear: 'I'm not thinking of getting married ...'

Maggie was serious now. 'His mother tribal woman, father a white man. He can read and write. Good with sheep, everything.'

Maydina looked sideways at Maggie, and she smiled a little. 'Maggie, you make me shame ...'

'No good woman to be alone. You have little girl. Must have someone look after you. That Joala, he right sign, right skin for you ...'

Maydina once more looked through the open door. Joala saw her, smiled and raised his hand. Maydina quickly turned away.

From then on her and Joala's eyes often met when they were all assembled for prayers in the bough shed; and once she watched him as he broke in a horse, and she was surprised how quickly the young animal trusted him.

In Maydina there began a faint stirring of new hope. When she walked, there was a spring to her step. The days with Alf the sealer slowly began to fade and became nothing more than a bad dream, a past which had to be forgotten.

There was only one thing that troubled her: Biri spent more and more time at the homestead. She spoke English better than her mother, and she was proud of it and showed it. Mrs McPhee seemed very pleased with her; she gave her numerous presents: coloured pictures of Jesus with children at his knees; pictures of angels, of people from the Bible. She gave her ribbons for her hair; she even made a frock for her and gave her a pair of shoes, so that she was dressed like a little white girl.

Once Maydina had seen Mrs McPhee and Biri sitting on a rug in the garden, drinking tea. They had laughed and joked. Maydina had never seen Mrs McPhee so cheerful and so happy. Maydina had felt a stab of jealousy; it was as if the white woman wanted to steal her child from her – the child that was part of her own body, of her spirit. She would not let her be taken.

One day, as she was about to rinse some sheets in the river, Mrs McPhee called out to her from the verandah. Biri and Johnny had finished their Bible lesson and were playing in the yard. They had sticks between their legs, with reins attached, and they pretended they were riding horses. Johnny was brandishing a wooden sword; Biri carried a flag with a cross on it: they were Crusaders, slaying heathens.

'Come here, May,' Mrs McPhee said briskly, 'and listen.' She turned to the children, and they came and stood in front of her, expectantly.

'Now!' Mrs McPhee looked at them keenly, 'Who were the first people in the garden of Eden?'

'Adam and Eve!'

'That's right. Who was in the lion's den?'

'Daniel!'

'Who was the strong man whose hair was cut off by a lady, and who lost his strength?'

'Samson!'

'Very good!' Mrs McPhee's face shone with pride and joy as she looked down at the children who beamed back at her. 'The Lord will be pleased with them.' Then she paused. She had noticed that Maydina did not smile, and she was disconcerted. 'Will he be pleased with you?' she asked. Something told her that she must spend more time with Maydina, must not neglect her for her daughter.

Maydina did not answer.

'Well, back to work; the Lord does not like idle hands . . .' Mrs McPhee turned and walked into the house. Maydina watched her go. She, too, could please the children.

'Come with me,' she said. The children left their toys and ran after her.

Soon the house and paddocks were behind them and they walked down a narrow pathway to the river. It was a narrow stream that ran between moss-coloured boulders, past ferns, past eucalypts, over pebbles, rocks, and smooth sand. A group of tiny thornbills with pale yellow breasts and green wings flitted about, calling to one another in their sweet, high-pitched voices. A wagtail chattered, turning this way and that, filled with his own importance. He would fly ahead a little, then sit down again, and look at Maydina with his sharp black eyes. Maydina smiled: he was a messenger. She wondered whose message it could be. She looked at Johnny, Joala's son. He was a handsome boy, full of life, only about six years old.

Soon Maydina stood in the water, bloomers rolled up as high as they would go, her frock hoisted around her hips. The children had taken off their socks and shoes and were playing in the water, splashing each other, and looking for pretty pebbles.

Maydina put the basket with the washing between two rocks underneath some fern, and they began to look for berries and for plants, which she collected in a kind of coolamon made of a piece of bark. Maydina explained to the children what things were good to eat, and where to find them; she told them how the old people used to hunt, how the echidna could be caught and the goanna. When they found a bee-hive in a hollow tree, Maydina made a fire by rubbing two sticks together, and they smoked out the bees and took some of their honey.

Later they sat together, dipping their fingers into the coolamon which held the honeycomb, and Maydina told them stories. 'You know,' she said, leaning against a tree, licking her fingers clean, 'little children must not go alone to water . . . Bunyip lives there . . .'

'What's he look like?' Johnny asked, his mouth dropping open.

Maydina began to describe the Bunyip with many gestures: 'Lives in water, big as mountain . . . got long hair . . . big, big hands . . . eats people . . . always looking for little girls and boys . . .'

The children giggled, not sure what to believe, and pleasant shivers ran up and down their spines.

They heard Maggie's voice call in the distance, and they answered. Then in silence they picked up their things – their shoes, their socks, the sheets – and went back to Balambool.

Mrs McPhee, after many anxious looks through the window, saw them coming, and now stood on the verandah steps. She had not known that the children had gone with Maydina, and had been greatly worried. She even thought of sending Old Tom after them – he was an expert tracker. Unable to understand how they could be so naughty, so disobedient, she thought she would have to punish them. Now she knew that it was Maydina's fault.

She looked at Maydina, and saw no trace of remorse, or guilt, or shame, or humility. She thought she even saw defiance.

'Maggie,' she said, 'take the children, clean them up.' Maggie took Biri's and Johnny's hands and led them away.

'I'll not punish them,' she said, and just managed to keep her voice from trembling, 'because it is you who has led them to this wickedness.' She stood straight and tall, hands clasped in front of her. 'You must not take the children without permission. It is forbidden, do you hear? You will receive no sugar and no tea till you are more obedient. As long as you live here you will do as you are told. I'll not have you upset the children. If you don't mend your ways you'll have to go, but I'll make sure that Emily stays with us.'

Maydina stared at her; she could think of only one thing to say: 'She my daughter. Biri – she my daughter!'

Mrs McPhee spoke, and her voice was shrill: 'Her name is Emily! And she'll move into the house.' She turned and walked away.

Maydina stood, the basket of washing on her hip. She did not know what to do.

During evening prayers Maydina sat in silence. Biri had been placed in the front row with Johnny, where Mrs McPhee could keep an eye on them. Mrs McPhee spoke of the sin of disobedience, and now and then she seemed close to tears. She did not look at Maydina.

Maydina did not listen; she thought of taking Biri and running away from Balambool. But where could she go? There was no safety anywhere. She wanted to leave so that she might not lose her daughter, but if she did they would both be lost.

Her eyes fell on the carving of Jesus on the cross. It had been painted white, but some of the paint had cracked, and one could see the dark wood underneath. She stared at it without really seeing it, and she felt helpless, cut off, and nothing in the world made any sense to her.

After service Mrs McPhee quickly took Biri with her to the house.

A bed had been prepared in an enclosed part of the back verandah. There was a small window which could not be opened, and the door led directly into the house. Above the bed there was a picture of a guardian angel. Mrs McPhee pointed it out to Biri who was very silent, awed, a touch uneasy. She understood that something significant was happening because of her; she wished she could be with her mother, yet, at the same time, she had also become attached to this white lady who had been good to her, and who seemed to know everything. It was a good feeling to be loved and to be singled out by someone who was so all-knowing, and so powerful. She was aware that Mrs McPhee preferred her even to Johnny.

Mrs McPhee helped Biri to undress and put on her nightgown; then they both knelt and said a short prayer. Biri got into bed, and Mrs McPhee tucked her in, and for a moment it looked as if she would stoop and kiss her. But she straightened and smiled and merely said 'Goodnight, dear child,' and left, taking the candle with her. And she locked the door.

Mrs McPhee was relieved that the child was now completely in her charge. Perhaps the incident that had upset her so much in the afternoon was all a part of God's plan. It was clear he had wanted her to take the child away from the mother's influence. Perhaps the punishment would even bring Maydina to her senses.

Now that she thought back, she felt there had always been something about Maydina that had worried her – a certain pride, a stubbornness. She was sure that the Devil was ensconced in the woman's soul, and she prayed that she might have the strength to drive him out.

Maydina had waited in her hut for the lights to go out in the house, and soon there was only a glow from the window of the outhouse where young Mr Edward had his bed. Maydina sneaked towards the homestead, to the back verandah, and she gently knocked against Biri's window. Biri was still awake, and she pressed her face against the glass. Maydina whispered endearments, and words of comfort in the language. Biri cried; she had never been separated from her mother, and she was used to snuggling up against her as she went to sleep.

At last Maydina turned away.

The moon was very bright, and everything stood out clearly. The leaves on the trees, the blades of grass – each one was streaked with silver. Far away a dingo howled and was answered by another.

In the shadow of a tree Maydina saw a man. She stopped, uncertain, apprehensive. He stepped out into the open: it was Joala. Maydina slowly, shyly, walked towards him.

'You bin good to my little Johnny,' Joala said.

Maydina smiled a little. She was still close to tears.

'He had good time with you, and your daughter . . .' Joala stood, lost for words.

Maydina nodded. 'He nice boy, your Johnny . . .'

Joala took something from his pocket, then handed her a small wooden bowl he had carved. 'Got this for you,' he said. Then he gave her a small wooden kangaroo. 'This one for Biri . . .'

Maydina held them in her hands. She did not know what to say.

Joala was worried. 'You like 'em?'

Of course she did. She nodded quickly. They began to walk under the trees.

'. . . You Christian?' Maydina asked. She could not believe he was.

Joala was serious. 'The Bible they talk about . . . that's blackfeller story, too. The Great Spirit was here long time before whitefeller got that story.'

Maydina looked down at her feet and was silent.

Joala smiled again. 'I'm Christian for Mrs Bee, keep her happy, but I don't forget my Law.'

'. . . Why you stay here, Joala?' Maydina asked at last.

'This my mother's country. One day I'll get some back.' He stopped and looked down at her. 'One day I'll build a house for myself, for wife, for children . . .'

Then they stood without saying anything, thinking about what had been said. There was a swishing sound – someone was walking past in a long skirt. A woman stepped from the shadows of the trees and made for Edward's room: it was Matilda, a girl who had been born here at Balambool and had been brought up with Mr Edward. It was known that the two were fond of each other, and the People smiled at it and kept it secret from Mrs McPhee.

Night lay over Balambool. The moon's light was on the homestead, the sheds, the paddocks, on the surrounding bush. Everything seemed tranquil, and at peace; but it was not so: the night was full of longing, of desire, hopes and fears, full of burgeoning life, of silent growing, of searching for fulfilment. A wagtail sang its song, and it was a sweet and haunting sound, but when the messenger sings at night it means the coming of some sadness.

Maydina, with Biri no longer in her care, spent much of her time in the area the late Mr McPhee had set aside for the people. The river was not far away, and the soil was sandy. A number of lean-tos, huts and mia-mias had been constructed here in the shelter of some trees. Soon Maydina would be shifting here from her place near the house, to live with Maggie and all the others.

The shelters were miserable: made of spare timber, branches, hessian bags and iron sheets. Few of them kept out the rain, none of them the cold. Still, Maydina and the others liked it here: here they could be themselves. They would sit around their fires, and they would talk of many things, and the past would become the present; old stories would be told, and there was laughter, singing, dancing. Sometimes Mr Edward would come visiting, and the men would teach him a few things, like reading the tracks of various animals. They would talk about the land, and it was clear that Edward, too, had come to love the hills and plains around Balambool.

Maydina learnt that Maggie's husband Tom was still keeping the sacred things that had been handed down from generation to generation. He kept them in a secret place, and when the time was right the initiated men would go to a place in the bush and there conduct the ancient rites the Law demanded to keep the land and all its creatures in a state of harmony.

Maydina did not see much of Biri. She met her at the house when she was called there for domestic duties, and she saw her, of course, when they all met for prayers at the bough shed twice a day. Maydina decided to be patient. Joala and she had talked about getting married – it would have to be done the Christian way – and living in a hut like the whitefellers did. Joala would get some land; he would have to write a letter for that purpose and it was good that he knew how to read and write. They would keep sheep and cattle, and Johnny and Biri would live with them.

Joala knew a good deal about the white man's way because he and Edward spent much time together, and when they worked they talked almost like friends. Maydina learnt that there were people more powerful than Alf, the sealer, and his mates, more powerful than the woman who had taken away her child: they were living in a distant place and were called 'the government'. They gave the shoes and clothes that people wore; they gave the rations – flour, tea, tobacco – that Mrs McPhee handed out to them each week; and they were the ones who could give Joala some land. Soon one of them would come to Balambool – as was the custom once a year.

The first inkling that he was to arrive came when Maggie, Maydina and Matilda were put to work to clean the house from top to bottom. It was always spick and span, but now there was yet another burst of scrubbing, polishing, washing, ironing. Mrs McPhee's eyes were everywhere and on everything.

Maydina did not mind: it meant she could be close to Biri. Biri, too, was set to work. She had to clean silver, dust and sweep. She did not like doing these things for any length of time, and sometimes Maydina would secretly do her share as well.

Outside little Johnny had to weed the garden, and the men repaired fences, whitewashed sheds and stables.

Maggie and Mrs McPhee were busy in the kitchen, cooking, baking; the smell overpowered even the fragrance of the roses that grew in front of the verandah.

At last, on a Sunday afternoon, a buggy could be seen approaching. It was the Reverend Bligh's. With him was a Mr Johnston. Maydina was surprised to see that he was quite young. He was short and chubby, and his face was very white and looked polished. He had small piercing eyes and, as he and the Reverend Bligh alighted from the buggy, they darted this way and that, like a bird's.

Mrs McPhee came hurrying from the house, dressed in her Sunday frock. She smiled and stretched out her arms, as if the Reverend were a long-lost friend, and not someone who called regularly once a month. Then she turned to Mr Johnston, and she became dignified and pleasant. Mr Bligh did the introductions, and she listened, head inclined to one side a little.

Edward hovered in the background, a slight, cold, smile on his lips, and when they all looked at him, he reluctantly stepped forward to shake Mr Johnston's hand. Mrs McPhee shot an anxious glance in his direction; she hoped he would behave and hide his true feelings. She knew he had no faith in men like Johnston, and that he did not like the vicar.

The group turned towards the house. Beyond them, near the kitchen door, Maydina could see Maggie, resplendent in a new frock and a starched apron, flanked by Johnny and by Biri who had a pink ribbon in her hair and wore a dress with frills. She had grown a little, and her dark skin and eyes and hair were a sharp contrast to the pale pink cloth.

Maydina glanced across the yard where Joala was unharnessing the vicar's piebald horse. Joala looked preoccupied. Maydina knew this was an important day, a day that would affect their future, and her mouth suddenly went dry at the thought of it. Today Joala would ask for some of his mother's land back.

Mrs McPhee had been exasperated when she had realized that the Board for the Protection of Aborigines had once more sent a different inspector to her place. It meant that she had yet again to convince a new man of the importance, of the value, of the absolute necessity, of her work at Balambool. She hoped she had not shown her feelings of disappointment, because it would have been unwise to offend: without the aid of the Board Balambool could not exist.

She poured tea into dainty cups, offered scones and cream and jam and, while everyone talked about the weather and the possibility of a late autumn, she studied the two visitors out of the corner of her eye. She wondered how much she could rely on the support of the Reverend George Bligh; she did not like him or trust him as much as the previous vicar. He was leaning back in his chair, his wavy beard rested on his chest, and he was looking at the scones he was about to eat. He had a passionate face: dark burning eyes under bushy brows, a strong nose, full red lips which were always moist. His voice was deep, and he managed to give everything he said the ring of significance.

He bit into a scone, chewed rapidly, swallowed, and then praised their quality. They were exquisite. They reminded him of home; his late wife used to make scones like that . . . they had the same delightful texture. He praised Mrs McPhee for bringing a piece of England to this hostile, savage land, and he stressed how he looked forward to each visit he made to Balambool.

The sky outside was a cloudless blue; one could see a small piece of it through the window, past the verandah post. Two blowflies had got trapped in the room and were flying against the glass. Mrs McPhee gestured to Edward, and he rose, took a fly swatter that was lying there, and disposed of them with such alacrity that Bligh paused momentarily in his speech and looked at him.

Mrs McPhee had been wondering how to guide the conversation to the subject that was dear to her. Yes, she said, yes, she too longed for England. It was indeed a lovely place, better than any other, except paradise. Still, the Lord worked in strange ways; she remembered how her dear late husband had often questioned his decision to emigrate to the Colony, until his eyes had suddenly been opened to the suffering of the natives. He had seen a young woman nearly dead after the station hands on a neighbouring property had had their way with her. He had put her in his buggy and brought her back to Balambool, despite the lewd laughter and remarks from the men, and the discouragement of the squatter. The young woman had died eventually, despite all the care bestowed on her, despite all the prayers, but it had seemed that, when the hour had come, the woman had died in peace. The Lord had revealed himself to her, and she had passed away with the word 'Jesus' on her lips.

It was then that she and her late husband had realized that the Lord had sent them here so that they could show the children of the wilderness the way to salvation. Were they not all God's children who had to be united around his throne in heaven?

Mrs McPhee paused, her cheeks flushed. Bligh had listened with an expression of indulgent tolerance. Johnston's face remained polite and blank.

When Mrs McPhee took a sip of tea, he mentioned that the government had built a Mission not far from Balambool – about forty miles or so – for the purpose of protection of the natives. No one was allowed to enter or to leave without a written permit from the manager, white men included.

'Excellent,' the vicar said, 'excellent'. He added pointedly, 'It'll put an end to temptation.'

Edward shot a quick glance at him, but Bligh was looking into his cup of tea before lifting it to his lips, and Edward did not know if the remark was meant for him.

Mrs McPhee had heard of the place, and she was not impressed. 'I hear the accommodation is quite pitiful,' she said, 'and the resident minister is negligent in his duties.'

Johnston smiled a little; he spoke carefully, not willing to upset his hostess. 'Well . . . it has been found,' he cleared his throat, 'that too much spiritual guidance has the opposite effect. It makes the natives rebellious, and they revert to their old ways . . .'

'Poppycock!' Her eyes flashed; she was ready to do battle. 'Mr Bligh will verify that the people in my charge are hardworking Christians! There is no sign of rebellion here!'

Not much later Mrs McPhee, Edward and the two visitors strolled down to where the people lived. Mrs McPhee had applied for assistance to build better shelters – solid huts – to house those she called 'her natives'.

Johnston looked around; he was not sure. Wasn't it true that the blacks were used to living in the open? Preferred it, even? Mrs McPhee shook her head. They caught colds, pneumonia, consumption and the whooping cough; she was anxious to have them housed decently. Too many had died the previous winter.

Maydina stood with the other women, next to Maggie and Matilda. They had all been briefly looked at by Johnston as he passed, hands behind his back. Maydina had had her eyes to the ground, but she raised them as she realized the visitors were now approaching the group of men where Joala stood. For a moment she felt fiercely proud. In her mind's eye she saw him as a warrior and a hunter. She noticed that Mrs McPhee, too, was proud of him; she pointed him out to the man from the government.

'Now,' she said, 'this is Charlie. He is our foreman. He is a fine example of what we are trying to achieve . . .'

Johnston gave Joala a fleeting smile, nodded and made to move on.

Joala stepped forward. 'I got something to say,' he said. His voice was hoarse. The others looked at him with some surprise. It had never happened that one of the people addressed a visitor, let alone one from the government. 'I've been working a long time for you now, Mrs Bee . . .' He twisted his hat in his hands.

Mrs McPhee felt flustered and uneasy, but she smiled. What could Charlie want? Why didn't he keep quiet? 'Yes,' she said, 'you have done well, and we are proud of you.'

'I want some land.'

There it was. A simple sentence. Four simple words. Joala was glad that he had spoken, and he looked at those before him. They were flabbergasted. For a moment nobody could think of anything to say. Then at last Johnston raised his eyebrows and said, 'Land? What for?'

'Want to be farmer.'

Johnston smiled a little, and spoke as if to a child. 'That's not as easy as you think.'

'I know. But I have learnt. Mrs Bee knows I work hard.'

He looked at her. She was confused; she was totally unprepared for this request. 'We wouldn't know what to do without you, Charlie,' she said at last and smiled, trying to make light of it.

In the background Bligh shook his head and clicked his tongue and muttered: 'Greed rears its ugly head . . .' as if he had expected something like this all along.

Mr Johnston chuckled. 'Mrs McPhee can't give you any land. She's barely got enough herself . . .'

Joala felt a surge of anger; his face became darker as the blood rushed to his cheeks, his eyes flared: 'Gub'mint took all the land.' He flung his arm wide. 'Took all this!'

Johnston's voice turned a trifle hard: 'If we gave you some, others would want it, too.' It was obvious the man was a mutineer. The question was how to handle him.

Mrs McPhee hastily intervened. She had never seen Joala like this, and it was most upsetting that he had chosen to speak out at this particular time. 'Charlie,' she said, almost pleadingly, 'you've got everything you need, you're happy here . . .'

Joala looked at her; he had no grudge against her. She had been good to him and to his little son, but he said stubbornly: 'This is my mother's country; so it's mine, too.'

There was a brief pause. The people had not moved; they stood and waited, their eyes on the white men and the white woman in front of them, in the sun.

High above them a wedgetailed eagle circled, its wings spread, almost motionless.

'Well, my good fellow,' Mr Johnston said at last, 'I suggest you compose a petition to the Colonial Secretary re acquisition of some acres. And when you've written it all down, give it to Mrs McPhee who will pass it on to me . . .'

He made to turn away, thinking that he had dealt with this matter, but Joala dug into his pocket and produced a small piece of paper. 'Here,' he held it out, 'I write something down . . .'

Johnston took the paper, looked at it, and smiled a little. 'Good,' he said, 'I'll see this is delivered.'

Maydina had not heard what had been said, but she had read the expressions. When Mrs McPhee and the men had turned their backs, she hurried across to Joala who stood, hands hanging by his side, staring at the ground. She looked at him anxiously.

He nodded grimly; he would get some land, though he hadn't liked the smile the whitefeller had given him.

When dinner had been served – roast lamb and baked potatoes – Mrs McPhee was anxious to hear what Johnston thought of Balambool. He said he was impressed but could not guarantee the kind of assistance Mrs McPhee had in mind. And besides, why should a lady burden herself with this kind of responsibility? Far better to let the government take care of things; the newly established Mission was the proper place, well equipped.

Mrs McPhee opened her mouth to speak, but Johnston quoted her foreman, Charlie, as an example. How could she be expected to deal with this kind of situation? Firm handling was required.

The vicar nodded, smiled. Yes, she had perhaps been too lenient, too gentle . . .

He caught Edward's eye, and saw a glint of hostility, of mockery. It stung him. He wished he could voice his suspicions about Edward's relationship with the native women.

'Who knows what these people think?' he said. 'They may well embrace the outward signs of Christianity, and still cling to their depraved and immoral ways. Their state before we came was lower than a beast's: they deliberately indulged in sinful practices: they are used to deceit . . .'

'How long have you been in this country, Mr Bligh?' Edward tried to speak calmly, but it was difficult.

'Long enough, young man, long enough.' He turned to Mrs McPhee, and the words poured forth: 'It disturbs me when I see them at the funerals, painted like pagan tribes . . . You must put an end to this, dear lady, you really must.'

Edward threw up his hands. 'Look! What does it matter? They aren't doing any harm! I've seen them do dances in the bush; it keeps them happy –' He stopped, and felt like biting off his tongue.

His mother stared at him; it was the first time she had heard of it, and she was horrified.

The vicar looked at her, and for a moment he was too shocked to speak. 'Were you aware of that?' he said at last.

She shook her head. 'If I had, I assure you it would have been stopped at once.' Johnston looked from one to the other: he did not share their real fear of Satan; rather he shared Edward's views, and he smiled to himself a little.

That night, when everyone was assembled at the bough shed, there was a feeling of tension in the air. Maydina saw not far from the entrance a large heap of wood stacked for a fire. No one knew what it was for, but Edward had acted oddly when he had asked Joala and some of the men to stack it; he had seemed impatient, irritable, as if he disliked what he had to do.

Mrs McPhee, too, was not her usual self as she sat down behind the pedal organ. The people had always seen her full of vigour, of vitality and fervour, when she came to conduct the service: she loved it, deriving great spiritual satisfaction from the singing and the prayers. Tonight she looked wan and shaken and subdued.

The Reverend George Bligh appeared, in contrast, taller than he was. He had the Bible clasped under one arm, and was swinging his walking cane in the other. He looked solemn and imposing and now and then he would fix the congregation with a stare.

When everyone was in place and there was silence, he stood under the lantern which was suspended from a beam, and in its light he read from the Bible, from a page that he had marked. His voice was low and even as he began: 'Revelation, chapter twenty-one.' He looked up to make sure that everyone was attentive. Then: 'He that overcometh shall inherit all things; and I will be his God. And he shall be my son.' Now his voice began to rise, and his finger pointed at the words he read: 'But the fearful, and the unbelieving, and the *abominable*, and the murderers, and warmongers, and *sorcerers* and all liars shall have their part in the lake which burneth like fire and brimstone, and which is the second *death*.' He ended, relishing the words, closed the book and looked up.

His audience were silent. The words meant nothing, but they heard the menace in his voice, and his face, half lit, half in shadow above the blackness of his suit, looked frightening with its red lips, sharp nose, burning eyes.

Bligh was satisfied with the response which, he believed, was the result of awe. He now spoke sternly, but as if he talked to children: 'It has come to my ears that you have been very disobedient . . . that you still follow your old and evil customs!' He stretched an arm in Mrs McPhee's direction, and went on, 'This lady has given much of her life in service to the church to make you Christians, but you? You cling to sin! To evil!' He grew more intense, and leaned forward, and shook his fist at them. 'You show no gratitude! No humility! You hold on to the instruments of Satan! I know you have hidden them in a secret spot!'

In the background Mrs McPhee sat, her eyes closed, hands clasped in prayer.

Bligh drew himself up to his full height, his eyes on those before him. After a long pause, he spoke imploringly, yet at the same time commandingly: 'I want you to bring these things to me.' Another pause. 'Charlie, light the fire . . .'

Joala went out to do what he was told, wondering what was to come.

The Reverend George Bligh had been convinced that God had called on him to exorcise the Devil. He was suddenly filled with fear as he looked at the congregation, the many dark faces in the shadows. He hated himself for his weakness, believing that this, too, was the work of Satan. His voice trembled slightly as he spoke more quietly: 'Together we shall burn the tools of the Devil. Mrs McPhee, music, please.'

Mrs McPhee was crying, but she played.

Outside the fire began to burn, and the flames spread a flickering light into the shadows of the bough shed.

Joala came back inside, and stood not far from where Maydina sat. Since Bligh had started talking, she had been watching Biri and Johnny who were in the front row and were terrified.

Bligh fixed his eyes on old Tom, whose real name was Yallaroi. 'Thomas,' he said, 'in the name of the Lord, bring these things to me.'

Yallaroi rose to his feet. His face was very calm, his voice quiet; he spoke with the dignity of a tribal elder: 'We cannot give them.'

Bligh stared at him; he had not expected this. He thundered 'Bring them here!'

Old Yallaroi did not move. Mrs McPhee stopped playing, and there was utter silence. Somewhere, a cicada began to chirp. Then Yallaroi spoke, and it was as if his voice was coming from far away: 'You have taken from us the land; here where our people once lived stands this place. Many of our people are dead.

But we are here, and these things you ask we cannot give: they belong to our people for a long long time . . .'

A vein began to swell in the vicar's face.

Yallaroi went on: 'They belong to our fathers, grandfathers, and their fathers; they belong to our children, and children's children, and children to come –'

'Witchcraft! Sorcery,' the vicar muttered fiercely.

'They carry the spirit of the land, and of the people.'

The vicar's face contorted; his voice rose to a shout: 'In the name of the Lord! Bring them to me!'

He lunged forward, grabbed his cane, dragged the old man towards him and threw him to the ground – with the strength of a man possessed. The people rose to their feet, amazed, horrified; some of the women screamed. Mrs McPhee got up, unable to believe her eyes.

The vicar, with all his strength, brought down the cane. He went on hitting the man at his feet, despite cries, shouts of anger and of outrage that were coming from all sides, till Edward and Mr Johnston held his arm and made him stop. Then he stood trembling, staring, not seeing anything. Behind him the wooden image of the crucified Christ seemed to float in the dark, arms outstretched, like a white shadow.

Maydina had rushed towards the children, took them by their hands, and ran out of the bough shed, past the blazing wood, into the night, away from the turmoil, the pandemonium, the horror.

She stopped near the stables, and saw that Joala had followed them. 'Where you going?' he asked, and already knew the answer. 'Get 'way from here,' she said wildly, 'Get away!'

Joala nodded. He was leaving, too.

Maydina got some blankets, and the rations she had earned; Joala fetched the rifle Edward had given him. With the children, who were still frightened and subdued, they went away into the night – towards the hills.

Mrs McPhee's first question after she and her visitors had returned to the house was: 'Where is Emily?' Nobody knew. No one had seen the child. Mrs McPhee wanted to go out and look for her, but was dissuaded. So she sent Maggie in her stead, and then half-heartedly attended to the vicar who after his outburst was exhausted, numb.

Mr Johnston had usurped authority and ordered all the windows closed, all doors locked and bolted: he expected rioting. Edward wryly obliged, and they sat as if they were under siege.

At last Maggie returned. The children were nowhere to be found; neither were Maydina and Joala. Mrs McPhee's worst fears were confirmed. She hurried to her room, threw herself on her knees and pleaded desperately with the Lord to protect Emily and Johnny, and to return them to her safely.

Joala and Maydina had lit a fire in a sheltered spot. The children, still in their Sunday clothes, went to sleep, wrapped in blankets. Maydina and Joala sat in silence for a long long time. After the wild scene at the bough shed the peace here was absolute. A small river was close by, and soon a mist began to rise, and they were cut off from the world, from time itself. At last the glow of the fire, too, seemed imprisoned by the mist; only the trunks of the closest trees were visible, their crowns merging with the dark.

Maydina could not think; her mind was still in chaos. But she knew that she had seen the Evil One. The Evil One who survived in no other living creature except in man himself. In a place that had appeared a refuge of some kind, he had come and gone, unrecognized, and then had revealed himself at last by wanting to destroy the Law. She wondered what had happened after she and Joala and the children had run away. Had he killed Old Yallaroi? Had he seized the sacred things and destroyed them? If so – what would happen?

Her eyes were on the children. Whatever the future held, it was good that they had left Balambool.

Morning came at last, the mist dissolved before the rising sun, the world was clean and fresh; kookaburras filled the air with their cackling, magpies sang. Maydina felt she had come home. How good it was to be among the things she knew, things that were part of her as she was part of them. As she sat there while Joala and the children were still sleeping, she felt the blood singing in her veins. Tears came to her eyes and ran down her face like a soothing stream.

The children stretched and yawned, and came to life. Maydina looked anxiously at them. Would they miss Mrs McPhee? Would they want to go back to Balambool? But they had eyes only for the glory of the morning. Joala caught some fish, and soon the smell of cooking on hot stones filled their nostrils.

Joala had done much thinking in the night. No longer would they be free to live in the old way, but they would find a place where there was good grass and much water, Joala would work for other people, and from them he would get in return some sheep and cattle. They would have a farm like the whitefellers had. Why should he ask the government? The government was far away and would never know. Besides, why must he beg land from them? The land was not theirs to give.

Maydina listened quietly, and thought his plan was good – but deep inside she still longed for the kind of freedom the people had enjoyed in the old days.

Like Maydina and Joala, Mrs McPhee had hardly slept at all. She saw in her mind's eye Emily assailed by a thousand dangers in the bush. She saw her bitten by a snake, falling down steep embankments, drowning. She saw her cold and lonely, crying for her as she was being dragged away. Emily had given her more pleasure than anyone she had ever known. How quick she was to learn! How cheerful! How beautiful were the large dark eyes! She had had such plans for her. She had decided that she would stay at Balambool for ever. Maydina, headstrong and stubborn as she was, had spoilt everything. Thanks to her, Emily would be without protection, would be at the mercy of those monstrous men who looked at the native women as a means only to satisfy their lust. And what if Emily should forget Jesus? If she ceased to be a Christian, then what hope was there for eternal life, for a meeting again in heaven?

She blamed Bligh for the tragedy, and she found that she could barely look at him. The two men had stayed on, and there had been much discussion. It was as if they had taken over

Balambool. Edward was no help. He was too young to assert himself, and so stood back, apparently deriving some satisfaction from the fact that his dislike for the vicar had been justified, and that he had been more correct in his assessment of Johnston than his mother. What did upset him was the fact that Joala had left. He was almost irreplaceable.

Mrs McPhee looked at the portrait of her late husband. If only he had been alive! Not only would he stand up to Bligh and Johnston, but he would also give her strength and guidance, because she could no longer make sense out of God's plans and reasons.

It had been decided that all the people at Balambool would go to the government Mission. 'The Lord knows what's best' – with these words the vicar considered the subject closed.

Mrs McPhee had to resign herself to it because without Johnston's support there was no hope for Balambool. 'All my dear husband's work has gone for nothing,' she said quietly. She walked to the window and looked into the yard where some of the people hovered. 'What will happen to these wretched souls when their journey through this vale of tears is over?'

'The Lord is at work,' the vicar said, and he got up from the table. 'He did not make the earth for savage tribes to wander over. It is the order of divine providence that those who stand in the way of honest labour and industry be scattered and swept away. We must accept with humility . . .'

Mrs McPhee was silent.

Maggie entered to clear the breakfast table. She did not look at anyone, but she felt pity for Mrs McPhee who, she knew, had meant well in her own way. She sensed that a change was in the air; after the incident the previous night nothing could ever be the same.

Johnston was outside, talking to a sergeant of police. He was determined that the fugitives be brought back; it would not do to have a native take his fate into his own hands – to defy the authorities.

Now he entered. 'Call the people together for a meeting at the bough shed,' he said to Maggie. 'Mrs McPhee wants to talk to them.'

Maggie unhurriedly picked up the tray and walked out. Johnston watched her, not sure if she had heard or not.

Maggie went to where the people had their shelters. Most of them were there; no work had been given out; the ordinary stream of life had been disrupted. Old Yallaroi was sitting in the shade of a tree, and one of the women put a soothing lotion on his bruised, lacerated back. When they heard what Maggie said, they slowly made their way to the bough shed.

They entered it reluctantly, remembering the evil that had happened here. They listened to Mrs McPhee, who looked haggard and unhappy, but told them bravely that they would be sent to the government Mission where they would learn a new kind of life. She implored them not to forget what she had taught, prayed that they would remain Christian, and that they would all meet again in the life hereafter. She broke down and cried, and many of the women also cried – because they felt in a strange way united with this white woman in her misery. And they had got used to Balambool: it had become a home.

Maydina and the others had set out for a place where Joala had spent some of his childhood days with his mother and her people. As they approached it, he pointed out to them the areas and landmarks he remembered. They kept away from the river flats where they could see sheep and cattle grazing, and made their way through land untouched by farming. Sometimes the going was not easy; the bush was thick, and and trees had fallen and lay across their path. Biri and Johnny soon grew tired, and so Joala and Maydina set up camp again. They did not think that anyone would follow them: they had done no wrong.

Biri wondered where they were going. Were they never to return to Balambool? The fearful scene at the bough shed had frightened her, but not enough to have a lasting effect. She had been happy at Balambool, and she did not understand why they had to leave. Maydina told her of the different life they would lead, and as she spoke she dreamt how it should be, and she began to believe in it herself. She trusted Joala. She had seen he knew much of the old ways; he was still at home here in the bush. Why should they not live free, in their own way? There still was much land where no white man had been.

Later Joala killed two ducks, and soon they had a fire burning. Maydina and Biri found wild berries which were good to eat.

While the ducks were roasting between hot stones, Joala made a small spear for Johnny, and Johnny started practising as soon as it was finished. He felt important and grown up – a warrior and a hunter.

The place was beautiful. Some large rocks provided shelter from the wind. A small river flowed close by; trees and shrubs surrounded the patch of grass. They thought it would be good to stay here for a while, to catch their breath, to have time to think.

And then they heard the sound of horses' hooves. It meant that white men were coming, and that there would be trouble. They would try and keep out of sight. But it was too late: through the trees they saw two white men in uniform. They were police. With them were two men of the people. They wore caps, like the whites, but they were dressed in red jackets. Joala knew what that meant: they were from a distant place, belonged to a different nation, and they were in the white man's pay to track and betray those of their own kind. There was no point in hiding.

The police had spurred on their horses the moment they caught sight of the small camp, and now came at them fast. 'Get the children,' the sergeant shouted. The troopers made for them.

Joala grabbed his rifle. 'Stop,' he roared. 'Leave them, or I'll shoot!'

The troopers hesitated briefly. Maydina held Biri and Johnny close to her and stood still – there was nowhere to run. The sergeant had moved towards them; a shot rang out; he yelled and clutched his arm, and almost fell from his rearing horse.

There was another shot; Joala fell back, arms spread wide, the rifle dropping from his hands. He lay still.

Maydina screamed and ran to him. She threw herself on him, and held him, and could not believe that he was dying. She pressed her hands against his wound as though she might stop the life from leaving him. The world, at peace just a short time ago, was now once more in chaos. The pain inside her was so great that she thought she herself would die; she raised her face towards the sky, and there came from her such a wail of grief that the whole bush fell silent.

The sergeant dismounted, his hand over his injury. One of the troopers grabbed the children who had been hiding behind a log. Maydina pulled them away from him. She stood, her arms around them, looking down at Joala. His eyes were still bright. She touched him. His body was still warm and supple. She could not accept that he was dead, and she called out to him, willing him to move, to turn his head, to look at her.

'Come on,' the sergeant said at last, 'you can do nothing for him now. Come on, let's go.'

They returned to Balambool.

Mrs McPhee was in the sitting room when Mr Johnston entered and told her that the fugitives had been caught. She looked through the window, and she was relieved and sent a prayer of thanks to the Lord when she saw the children. They were scruffy, tired, miserable, but they were unharmed.

She noticed that Charlie was not there, and she wondered what had happened, but she restrained herself and stayed in the house, waiting for the sergeant to report.

Not much later he came into the room, in company of the Reverend George Bligh who had asked for his horse and buggy: he and Mr Johnston were about to leave.

The sergeant was well satisfied with his mission. The injury was superficial, a flesh wound, nothing much. He was tough; it was all part of his duty. The foreman, Charlie, regrettably had had to be shot. It was in self-defence. He had fired the moment they had arrived on the site. But that's the way it goes: you couldn't trust the blacks.

Mrs McPhee was shocked: she had always thought Charlie a gentleman. Still, she had no desire to argue with the men. Besides, she was not sure . . . had they not betrayed her by following their pagan customs here at Balambool? She was now anxious to take the children, have them cleaned and fed, and put to bed.

'Ah, yes . . . ' the vicar said, 'what are your plans for them?'

Mrs McPhee was in a flurry; she knew she'd have to pitch her will against the vicar's and against Mr Johnston's. She felt inadequate. 'I must have time to think,' she answered and stood stiffly, hands clasped in front of her waist.

Johnston and the vicar exchanged a quick glance, then Johnston said: 'Mr Bligh and I have discussed the matter; we consider it best for me to take the girl to the Cootamundra Training Home. There she will learn domestic duties. The boy can be looked after at the Kinchila Home for Youngsters.'

'I would prefer to keep them here.' Mrs McPhee managed to keep her voice from trembling.

The men did not think this was a good idea. They pointed out to her that Maydina, knowing the children to be at Balambool, would escape from the government Mission where she would be sent with the others, and was bound once more to kidnap them. The trouble was that the natives did not know what was best for them; one had to be cruel to be kind. She – Maydina – must never know where the children had been placed. The vicar reminded Mrs McPhee that there was nothing more important than to make sure the two young souls would be saved – so that they were assured of entrance into heaven. It was essential that they be kept away from tribal influence. Was she prepared to take on this responsibility? What if she failed? How would she feel on Judgement Day?

Mrs McPhee could not think of anything to say.

Maydina crouched on the verandah steps while her own and the children's future was discussed in the living room. Her mind was numb from the events of the previous days, and she simply sat, staring into space, not seeing, not hearing anything. Maggie had warmed some broth in the kitchen and was about to feed her and the children when Johnston and Bligh emerged from the house and made for the buggy.

At the same time the sergeant and the constable seized the children and half dragged, half carried them away. Maydina found herself held by the troopers. As in a dream, a nightmare, she saw the children, bewildered and crying, put into the buggy. She called out to them, struggled against the hands which had grabbed her arms.

The buggy began to move; the vicar flicked his whip, the horse broke into a canter as the troopers let go of her, and she began to run.

She ran and ran, knowing there was no hope, but still running till her lungs gave out. She fell to the ground, and there, arms outstretched, she lay and cried, her tears darkening the dry soil.

N e r i d a,
the Waterlily

She had handed in her notice and left Melbourne on the first train in the morning. Got to Quidong about midday. And now she had been walking for an hour.

The road seemed endless. There was nothing to tell how far you had come. No landmark. Not a thing. Just barbed-wire fences, and a few dead trees on the right. There weren't even any sheep and cattle to look at: those that had survived the drought were agisted in other parts of the state, or had been sent to the abattoirs.

She tried to cheer herself up by thinking of the welcome she would get. Even that thought turned sour. She had always seen herself come home in triumph: the girl from Koomalah Mission who had made good, become a book-keeper instead of slaving as a domestic. They had all had such faith in her. Mum, Dad, her brother, Gran . . . they had been so sure she'd make it in a white man's world . . .

Now she wasn't sure that she wanted to. Why try and be like a gubbah? What did they have to be proud of? Look at the mess everything was in! They had thought they knew all the answers, but now even many whitefellers were having a tough time. If you were koori, what chance did you have of finding a job? – except, if you were lucky, cleaning up whitefeller's dirt? None at all.

She was tired of battling in a world where no one wanted her. That's why she had decided to go back home. She'd give them all a surprise. It would be good to be among people you loved. Who loved you. She could feel tears welling up, and for a while she just walked along and cried. She didn't make a sound, just let the water flow out of her eyes.

Then she pulled herself together. No good feeling sorry for herself.

Better see the funny side of things. Here she was, dressed like a gubbah – hat with feather, floral dress, high-heeled shoes – lugging her suitcase and handbag and cardigan along in the middle of nowhere in the blazing sun. Who was she trying to impress? The crows? ... High-heeled shoes! Whoever invented them? She felt like kicking them off and flinging them into one of the paddocks and walking on in her bare feet. She'd have to take off her stockings as well. The trouble was that she wasn't used to it any more, and the road had a lot of loose gravel on it. She could feel the blisters coming. And she was getting thirsty. If only there was a bit of shade somewhere, and a cool creek, to bathe your feet, wash your face ...

She squinted: the country around here looked desolate and depressing. She felt that it reflected her own soul, her spirit. She wondered what it had been like around here a hundred years ago. She could picture it lightly timbered, with delicate gums, and some big trees here and there. It would have been covered with fine native grass. Kangaroos, wallabies would have been grazing, and there would have been many birds ... How little time it had taken to change it! Now there was nothing but dust.

Yesterday morning she had waited outside a small factory which made workers' uniforms. She had been standing in the small lane, and she had looked at all the rubbish lying around – newspapers, bottles, an upturned garbage can. A small dog had been rummaging through the contents. Dogs shouldn't have to be in places like that. Come to think of it – she smiled bitterly – nobody should. Not even humans.

For a few moments she had a vision of all the offices, shops, warehouses, factories she had been to since finishing her book-keeping course. They had all been so drab. So ugly. In a way the ugliness of the devastated landscape was like the ugliness in the city: the places did not have a soul.

Another girl had turned up for the job in the factory. Bleached hair, big bosom. She hadn't made an appointment, had come just on the offchance. She had been good-natured, easy-going, friendly. There had even been some feeling of sisterhood between them for a start – despite the fact that they had come for the same job. They had laughed when they had found out they'd been to the same business college – though at different times. They swapped notes about one of the tutors who hadn't been able to keep his hands to himself.

Then the girl had asked if she was a 'spaghetti eater'. Nerida had got used to the fact that people often thought she was Italian or Greek; most of the koories were tucked out of sight on the reserves and no one ever expected to meet one of them, least of all one who could do book-keeping. Nerida always made a point of telling the truth – and she had started to get some weird kind of kick out of seeing the reaction. It was always the same: people stared, uncertain. The conversation would dry up. It was as if they had been told they were talking to a leper. This girl even stepped back – as if she were scared of catching something.

The factory manager didn't have to be told. He somehow knew straight away. He didn't even ask her into the office. 'Sorry, we don't employ Abos here,' he had said. 'Company policy.' And he had been quite polite when he had said it – which made it worse. You wondered if he knew how offensive the word 'Abo' was.

There was the sound of a car. Nerida turned around briefly and saw it approaching in a cloud of dust. She wasn't happy about it: she felt exposed and vulnerable here on the open road, with nowhere to run, nowhere to hide. She would hate it just passing and leaving her behind like so much dirt; and she would hate it to stop and someone leering at her and offering her a lift, and then making a pass at her. Why did it have to be there at all?

She walked on, looking straight ahead, trying to look confident and purposeful despite these ludicrous shoes of hers and the weight of the suitcase she was carrying.

The car slowed down, but she didn't look. She pretended it wasn't there. She heard the wheels crunch on the gravel, and she noticed out of the corner of her eye that it was an old battered utility, with a dog in the back. She could feel the driver's eyes sizing her up.

'Want a lift?' The voice was male, nasal, friendly, just a touch boisterous. It sounded like an old man's voice.

'No, thanks,' she muttered.

The car cruised along next to her. There was a chuckle now: 'Don't yer know me, girl? Jack Reilly. Boonal Station!'

Now she cast a quick glance into the car. Yes, that's who it was. He looked at her out of the shadow in the cabin, his face leathery, full of lines, his eyes pale blue, a very old battered felt hat on his head. Though he was in his sixties, he still had the innocence of a child. Her father and her brother had worked for Reilly during shearing time; he was all right.

He beamed at her and leaned across to open the door. 'Hop in,' he said, 'put yer case in the back. The dog won't bite yer. Too old, like his boss . . .' Another chuckle. He was pleased with himself, pleased with the world, pleased to have company.

Nerida did what he said. When the car started moving again, she surreptitiously slipped off her shoes, wriggled her toes. After that she simply let her mind float, while Reilly did all the talking. His voice just rambled on, slowly, cheerfully . . . all you had to do was make a few sounds to show you were listening. First it was the weather, and the drought which had hit the country real bad. Still, it couldn't last forever, could it? Then he wondered how things were in Melbourne, and he knew the answer: yes, things were tough. They were tough everywhere. No work. It was bad when a man couldn't find work. Worst thing that could happen to a bloke . . . 'Still, things ought to get better now,' he said cheerfully, 'with the war starting up in Europe. Australia, she'll do her bit. Bound to. Always did.' His voice was proud now. If he was young – yes, he'd join up again, be in it like a shot. You had to rally round when the country called . . . best country in the world. Free. That was the great thing about it. And it had to stay that way, my word . . .

Nerida didn't comment. He was a good man, but naive. Everything seemed so simple to him. He asked if her brother was going to enlist – like her father had first time round. Nerida said she didn't know.

At last he pulled up at the gate of Koomalah Government Mission. She thanked him, got out, took the case from the back of the ute; he blew his horn and drove off in a cloud of dust.

She turned. There was a sign at the gate: 'No entry without a written permit.' She walked past it into the Mission.

Her mother stared at her for a moment, in complete disbelief, as Nerida walked into the kitchen; she dropped the bucket she was holding, and flung her arms around Nerida, hugged her and laughed and cried, all at the same time. Then all the others came in, wondering what was going on, and there was more hugging and kissing and laughing and crying, and it was as if the sun had come up in that small house where the Andersons lived.

Later they sat on the little verandah out the back, having a cup of tea. They wanted to know all about Melbourne – nothing much had happened here at the Mission, nothing worth talking about, anyway – and Nerida told them how she had been trying to get a book-keeping job. It was funny: she could now laugh about the things that had happened to her. She described some of the managers and prospective bosses she'd met: now their pomposity, their arrogance, appeared ludicrous, quite farcical. The others chuckled with her. Even her father smiled, and shook his head.

'Never mind,' her brother said, 'They don't know what they're missing out on: the only accountant who can make bandicoot sandwiches . . .' But behind the joke there was an edge. She looked at him. He had become a young man in the last two years; he wasn't a kid any more. He was handsome. There was something restless about him, something explosive. What chance did he have here in this place, cut off from the rest of the world? He had the brains to be someone important. A poet, an engineer. A doctor even. Instead he was shearing sheep, digging ditches, picking fruit. The only education he'd ever had was here on the Mission, and that hadn't been much.

She herself had been lucky; she had been taken in by an aunt who lived in Melbourne, married to a white man; so she had been able to go to a convent when she was in her teens. She had a better education than most other koories she knew. Much help it was now!

When Mrs Felton turned up, Nerida's brother and father made themselves scarce. Mrs Felton was the manager's wife. Every fortnight she came round, checking all the houses – to see if the furniture had been dusted, sheets washed, blankets aired. Ivy, Nerida's mother, was finicky about cleanliness; everything was always spick and span. But what if she had wanted it dirty? If she thought it didn't matter? That was her right, wasn't it? There were plenty of whitefellers who never had a decent wash, whose houses were in a mess. Nobody checked on them! The gubbahs said it was necessary because the houses on the Mission were Government Property. Well, what about the government doing their bit? Fix up the cracks in the houses, for instance! They were large enough to put your hand in.

The worst thing was to see her mother's reaction when Mrs Felton called from the front door in a high-pitched voice and marched into the house without waiting to be asked. Ivy immediately was nervous, apprehensive – as if she had done something wrong. Why should she have to feel like that? Her mother was the kindest, gentlest person Nerida had ever known. Why should she feel inferior to anyone?

Ivy hurried into the house, the two men vanished through the hole in the back fence. Nerida sat, staring in front of herself. She felt her grandmother's eyes on her. She raised her own, and suddenly she had the feeling that the old woman was expecting her to do something. Something that was important. She didn't say anything; she just sat there and looked at Nerida. She had a powerful face: dark, her eyes were deep-set; she had a strong jaw, firm mouth. It was as if she had been hewn out of a dark rock. It was a moment Nerida would not forget: it made her think that the two of them were part of something that reached a long way back, long long into the past. It united them; they were two of a kind.

In the background they could hear Mrs Felton's voice: 'Dusted all these on top?' She spoke as if talking to a child – a half-deaf one at that. They heard Ivy replying, but they couldn't make out the words.

'Why does she put up with her?' Nerida asked hotly. 'They got no right to come in here like that . . .'

Her grandmother didn't answer for a moment or two. Then she shrugged. 'It's all thanks to the new manager; he's a little man with big ideas . . .'

Now Mrs Felton strode into the yard, followed by Ivy. She had been a matron in a hospital before she and her husband had come to Koomalah, and you could imagine her putting the fear of God into all her patients. She was middle-aged, bony. Her hair was pulled away from her face into a bun at the back. She had a ledger under her arm, and a pencil in her hand. She looked at the blankets hanging on the washing line. 'One, two, three, four . . .' – she looked into the ledger – 'I thought we had you down for five?'

'There's four,' Ivy said in a low voice. 'One for each person.'

Mrs Felton, still apparently dubious, nevertheless ticked off the items in the ledger, then briefly, in passing, acknowledged Grandmother's presence.

Her eyes fell on Nerida. 'Who are you?'

Nerida could not bring herself to answer.

'That's my daughter, Nerida, she's just come 'ome . . .' Ivy said quickly. She dropped her 'H's when she was nervous and put them in places where they didn't belong.

Mrs Felton still stared at Nerida. 'Have you a permit to come onto the Mission?'

'No.'

'You go and see the Manager straight away.'

'I'll have a bit of a rest first, Mrs Felton,' Nerida said icily, but as calmly as she could. But Mrs Felton sensed her hostility, her defiance.

'You must know the rules, Nerida . . .' she was threatening now, though her voice too was quiet.

Ivy hastily intervened. 'Yes, she does,' she said, 'I'll make sure she comes hup.'

Nerida did not look at her mother, but she felt a wave of exasperation. Why was her mother so humble, almost servile! Why didn't she show some resentment, some pride! The trouble was that she was a real Christian. She was a better Christian than any gubbah Nerida had ever met. She always turned the other cheek. Never seemed to hate any one. If you were that gentle, Nerida thought, people kicked you even harder. She had seen it happen.

Mrs Felton left. Nerida had another cup of tea, and Ron and her father came back and they all had another chat. Ivy was getting more and more nervous, until Nerida, more for her mother's sake than her own, set out for the manager's house. Ron gave her company.

It was getting dark, and the small houses looked quite homely with the glow of the kerosine lamps behind the windows. In the failing light you couldn't see how dilapidated they were. People were sitting on the verandahs here and there, and some children played in the dust. Some of the people recognized Nerida, and they wondered if she'd come home for a holiday. No, no, she had come home for good . . . They were pleased to see her, and friendly, but somehow they made her feel like a stranger. She had seen a little of the world outside, but the people here were cut off; they didn't know what was going on outside Koomalah. They were like prisoners here, and life was passing them by. Nerida's heart grew heavy; she didn't think she would be able to bear staying here for any length of time, despite her love for her family. Where could she go? What could she do? There was no answer.

The manager's house stood in a garden in which the lawn was dying and a few roses and rhododendrons were struggling to survive. It was quite large, and it had a new coat of paint – pink – which made it stand out in the dusk.

Felton was having his tea. Nerida caught a glimpse of him as Mrs Felton opened the kitchen door and told her to wait. She was told she wasn't to come up on the verandah: there was a bell at the bottom of the steps; she should ring next time she wanted something – that's what it was for. No one was allowed up on the verandah. The door shut in Nerida's face.

She and Ron sat down on the steps and waited. Finally Felton emerged from the kitchen. The fly-wire door banged shut; he stood there, hitching up his pants, and belched. Then he came down the steps. He was a big man, going flabby. He wore slippers. But you could see he'd once been in the Army: it was in the way he carried his shoulders.

He walked past them towards the door which had a sign with 'Office' written on it. Ron and Nerida made to follow him, but he jerked his head at Ron: 'Not you. Wait here.' Ron hung back.

When Felton turned on the light in the office, Nerida briefly saw him properly for the first time. He was middle-aged, and there were signs that he was on the bottle. There was a redness around his nose, and the pores in his skin were large. Sure enough, in the corner next to the filing cabinet was a case with beer. A dirty glass stood on the desk; two flies had drowned in the dregs.

He hadn't looked at Nerida. He was rummaging through the filing cabinet which was in a mess.

'Shut the door.'

Nerida shut the door. A hot northerly had begun to blow, and a loose piece of metal made a scraping, squeaking noise somewhere. Felton was still looking for her file, and all she could see now was his back. His hair was very short, his ears stuck out.

Above him was a picture of the King and the Queen, under two crossed Australian flags.

Nerida suddenly felt oddly isolated – as if the world outside had ceased to exist, and as if she and Felton had been thrown together by a quirk of fate.

He'd found the file and threw it on the desk, then sat down. He studied her, and she could see she had made an impression. He opened the folder, glanced through some notes. 'I see you haven't spent much time at the Mission,' he said. 'Like the bright lights, do you?' She didn't answer. He leant back.

'What did you do in Melbourne?'

'I worked.'

'And why are you here now? Got the sack?' He chuckled.

'I resigned.'

'Love-life not good enough, eh?' He didn't smile when he said it, and his eyes were fixed on her.

She didn't respond. It was best to ignore that type of remark. She had met his kind before. More than once.

'Well,' he said then, 'you can make yourself useful here. Tidy up, do the chores. Maizie comes here three times a week, you can do it the other days . . .' He went on, not expecting her to comment: 'I'll pay you in rations: to the sum of three and sixpence per week.'

Her eyes narrowed slightly as she stood there and looked down on him. 'I'd rather do book-keeping, Mr Felton.'

He gaped for a moment, then checked his notes. 'Book-keeping? I've got you down as a domestic.'

'I did a course in evening classes.'

'Good for you.' He closed the file. He felt just a little unsettled. A book-keeper! He was way behind with his accounts. It would be nice to have someone bringing them up to date. On the other hand, he hadn't always been strictly honest . . . He'd have to make sure she kept her nose out of them.

On their way home Ron filled Nerida in about Felton. It was obvious that he had no qualification to run the Mission; he didn't know the first thing about agriculture. The place was going to ruin; nothing was being done. The machinery was rusting and idle, the cows gave no milk, the pasture was nothing but weeds. The people were powerless; Felton was not prepared to listen. He blamed the whole state of affairs on the weather.

He had supposedly opened a trust fund for the workers, but nobody had ever seen a single farthing of it. Nerida listened. She had heard things were similar on other reserves, and there was a lot of unrest. Had anybody ever done anything about it here at Koomalah? Challenged Felton? Complained about him to the Protection Board?

Ron shook his head. What good would that do? They didn't care. Anyway, Felton had his spies: young Peter and Eddie. They reported to him what was going on. Felton could throw anyone off the Mission, and no questions asked. Then what? There was no work anywhere. You'd be separated from all those you cared about, couldn't ever see them again because it would be up to Felton to give you a permit to visit. How would you live? There was no work for koories; she'd found that out herself. And join the Army? There was a recruiting poster up at the store: some white-feller slipping into a uniform. It said: 'Join the A.I.F. This is serious. Enlist now.' No way. Let them fight their own wars.

As they walked side by side, Nerida thought suddenly how beautiful it was to have a brother. She remembered when they had been kids; she was a few years older than he, and, in a way, she had helped to bring him up. Koomalah had been a good place to live in then ... They had built their own little community here; the manager then had been an Indian and he had under-stood the koories much better than any of the whitefellers that followed. Once there had even been a chance that her father and a few others would get a bit of land of their own. No hope of that any more ...

It was dark by now, and the stars had come out. Here, above the flat, barren land, the sky was enormous. She walked, looking up at it – like she had done when she was a child. Grandmother had told her a story once – about the stars dancing in harmony to the song of someone whose name she had forgotten.

When they got home, Ivy was preparing the evening meal. She was making roti out of flour and water, and used a bottle for a rolling pin. 'There's that many weevils in the flour ... you think it'll crawl away,' she said.

Grandmother grunted. She sat in her rocking chair, unravel-ling an old jumper.

The kitchen was very small. A kerosine lamp burned on the table, another on the shelf above the wood stove. Ivy, always wanting to make things look nice, had put a strip of newspaper round the shelf, cut in a pattern, so that it looked a bit like lace. Some of the decoration was missing: Dad sometimes pinched some of it when he needed paper to roll himself a smoke and he couldn't find anything else handy.

He was sitting next to the stove, all hunched up, one leg pulled up and crossing the other, elbow on his knee, smoking.

103

Grandmother and Ivy kept on telling him he should give it away, he'd die with all that smoking, but he said he'd die without it. He had his hat on his head. He hardly ever took it off. He said it kept him warm with all the cracks in the walls. Nerida looked at him lovingly: how thin he had become! And he was coughing a lot. His lungs had been affected when he was a soldier in France – when gas had been used in the fighting; and now it looked as if he had caught TB, like many others at Koomalah.

A voice was singing out: 'Anybody home?'

It was Rachel and her son Andy. Rachel had heard Nerida had come back to Koomalah and she had to see her. She threw her arms around her, hugging her, then stood back to look at her, and hugged her again. She couldn't stop admiring her and uttering little cries of amazement. How lovely she had turned out! She kept on looking at her son for confirmation. He hovered in the background and said little, but he smiled a lot.

'You got to be careful what you say in front of Andy now,' Ron grinned from ear to ear, 'he's a preacher now . . .'

Rachel was very proud. 'Yes, he's just graduated from Bible class.'

Nerida and Andy had grown up together, but they hadn't met each other for the last few years. Nerida was surprised to see him; he had grown tall, and his face was strong and kind. He looked more like an athlete than a clergyman.

'We've just been to see Mr Short,' Rachel said confidently, 'he's the pastor who's here till Andy takes over . . .'

So that's why she was dressed in her Sunday best. She wore her floral dress, and she had on a hat with two roses. Every time she moved, they quivered.

'You going to stay for tea?' Ivy asked.

'You mightn't have enough . . .'

But Ivy didn't take 'no' for an answer. Rachel was her best friend. If she was running out of anything, Rachel would help her out.

A little later they all sat round the table, and the mood was festive because Nerida had come home.

Suddenly Rachel leant back in her chair and looked at the others. 'Do you know what Mr Short had for his tea?'

The others waited.

'A potato.'

'A potato?' Ivy was staggered.

Rachel nodded. 'Nothing else.'

'Fancy the church letting him starve like that!' Grandmother was not impressed.

'Why doesn't he get a couple of bunnies?' Ron didn't feel sorry, either. 'Let's show him how we get our food . . .'

'Can't expect a pastor to go rabbitin', Ron!' Ivy clicked her tongue in disapproval.

Rachel agreed. 'No, you can't. I think we ought to visit Ida, and Marg, and May; ask them to give something. Church has always helped us when we was in need . . .'

Grandmother snorted. 'Well, where are they now?'

Grandmother belonged to a different time. She still remembered the old ways, though she herself had not been able to live them properly. But she could still speak the language. She had been taught by her mother and her grandmother, and no missionary had ever found out. It seemed to Nerida, as she looked at her, that the old woman possessed a secret, something that gave her pride and dignity and self-esteem that nobody could shake.

That night, when they all had gone to bed, Nerida asked her about the story of the stars. She shared her grandmother's room, and once again she felt like a child as she lay on the narrow bed and listened how the flying foxes carried Priepriggie, the great hunter and song-maker, up into the sky. There he was now, and the stars, which had been in chaos until then, began to dance to his music and were in harmony. Now that she was grown up she could see a meaning in this story she had not found there before.

Every night from now on she and Grandmother would talk about the way the old people lived and thought. It was as if a whole new world suddenly opened in front of her. Till now Nerida had always wanted to respect her heritage, but she had not found a reason for it. She had never realized how much wisdom, how much depth, there was in the old people's thinking. In the world outside there were no other values but those of the whitefellers. Even in the convent – though the nuns had been kind – she was given to understand that she came from an inferior race which was doomed to die. There had been affection and compassion, but it seemed that – unless you became like a white girl – you were of little value.

Three times a week Nerida went to the manager's house, and she scrubbed the floors and cleaned the windows, did the washing and the ironing. Everything was spotless; clean things were cleaned again. There was not enough work otherwise to keep Maizie and Nerida busy, but Mrs Felton made sure that the two were not sitting around doing nothing. Only Felton's office was never cleaned out properly; Mrs Felton did not like the girls to spend much time in there.

Mrs Felton knew very well what was going on. In the early days she had called her husband an adulterer, and there had been violent outbursts on her part. Felton simply shrugged off her accusations, declared she was imagining things. She had stopped sleeping with him. Not that she minded; she had always found sex rather awkward and disgusting. Now, realizing what he was up to with the blacks, she was nauseated at the thought of it. It confirmed what she had begun to suspect some time ago: her husband was a deviant; he was vulgar and uncouth. She could barely look at the women on the Mission when she went on her inspection tours. She felt they were laughing about her behind her back because of her being married to such a man.

Nerida and her mother would discuss her sometimes. Ivy felt sorry for Mrs Felton. She didn't have anyone with whom she could be friends; there was no white woman around for miles. No one had ever seen her cheerful. How miserable she must be! Nerida had no sympathy whatsoever. Why didn't she go back to Melbourne? She'd have company there; there were plenty like her around.

Mrs Felton could feel Nerida's defiance and hostility, though Nerida hardly ever spoke and did what she was told. Maizie didn't bother her as much; she was just a little slut who took advantage of the situation. But Nerida – she had class. Mrs Felton was determined to keep her in her place, made her clean bathroom and toilets, made her tidy up under the house. She tried to be at home on the days Nerida was up at the house, to keep an eye on things.

Thank God for Mr Short. Mrs Felton felt he was the only person she could talk to as an equal. He understood her; he appreciated why she was so strict. He, she saw with satisfaction, seemed to avoid her husband's company. He went to Quidong once a week, and it had become routine that she went with him – to do some shopping, go to the hairdresser, or the dentist. She looked forward to these outings, the rides in the old but well-kept car, the conversations. They were her only entertainment, and she was determined not to give them up.

When Mr Short had to change his visit from a Thursday to a Friday, she was faced with a dilemma. Friday was Nerida's day at the house. After some fretting and worrying she decided that she would take the risk. What did it really matter? Felton had had his way with so many women – one more didn't really count.

The moment Nerida realized that Mrs Felton was going out, she was apprehensive. When she had left, she tried to keep out of Felton's sight. She had never imagined that she could ever miss Mrs Felton, but now she prayed for her to come back soon.

Felton did his rounds, then went to his office. After a while Eddie and Peter, Felton's spies, turned up. They were Ron's age, and Nerida wondered what could make them side with a man like Felton. They sneaked past her as she was doing the washing in the laundry. They didn't look at her, as if they hoped that this, in turn, would make them invisible to her. Felton had seen them coming and now stood at the door, beaming, very jovial. She knew he would give them a beer – though it was against the law to give blacks a drink.

She was hanging up the washing by the time they left.

Felton farewelled them, then stood in the doorway of his office. She could feel his eyes on her, and she felt naked and vulnerable, and afraid.

When he called her, she pretended she hadn't heard. He called once more. 'Come here!' It was an order.

She turned; he beckoned with a nod of his head and walked back into his office.

She slowly followed. She was determined to resist somehow.

When she entered the office, he shut the door behind her, chuckled, and walked to his desk. 'So your brother wants to be a big shot, does he . . .'

She was thrown. What made him say this about Ron? Did Eddie and Peter tell him something about her brother?

'Seems to run in the family . . .' He grinned at her: 'Qualified book-keeper, eh.' He threw a ledger on the desk, opened it. 'Let's see how good you are.'

'I haven't finished my other work yet . . .'

'Never mind. Come on. Sit down, sit down.' He was quite cheerful.

She sat down in Felton's chair and stared at the open ledger. Nothing made any sense in it; she felt utterly helpless, frightened. In front of her were three empty glasses.

Felton was enjoying himself. He thought she was being coy; a lot of these women were a bit shy for a start. Only natural, he supposed.

'Well? Figures correct?' His voice was suddenly low and hoarse.

Nerida prayed inwardly that someone would come into the office. Nobody did. 'It looks all right,' she murmured at last.

'Isn't that good . . .'

He had moved closer, as if to look over her shoulder, and now she could feel his hand on the nape of her neck. She moved away, got to her feet, but he barred her way. With one hand he was undoing his trouser belt, with the other he was leaning against the wall to stop her from getting past. His face was red and sweaty, and very close. 'You can do your family a lot of good – or a lot of harm – specially your brother . . .'

She tried to dodge past him, beneath his arm; he grabbed her, forced her against the wall. His pants were slipping as he tried to get his mouth over hers. Finally she broke free, and when he tried to get hold of her again, she hit him in the face.

For a moment, she stood – horrified. What had she done? Attacked the manager! He was furious now, lunged at her, grabbed her blouse, tried to get her across the desk –

'Frank!'

Mrs Felton stood in the doorway. Behind her was Mr Short. He was shocked, embarrassed, didn't know where to look.

Nerida hardly noticed him; she was so glad Mrs Felton was there. She pulled her torn blouse together, close to tears with shame and hurt, unable to think of anything to say.

'Get out!'

Mrs Felton stood there, stiff and straight, clutching her hand-bag. It only came to Nerida now that Mrs Felton may have thought she had been a willing party.

'Mrs Felton . . .'

'Will you get out of here!' Mrs Felton was white with rage. Nerida hurried past her, past Mr Short who hastily stepped aside, and ran back home.

She didn't tell her mother and father what had happened, but they could guess when they saw the state she was in. They didn't ask any questions. Ron did, when they were alone. It was just as well Felton was up at the house and not anywhere near: Ron would have killed him.

Then Mr Short turned up. He and Nerida sat on the small back verandah, and Ivy fussed and brought them cups of tea. She loved looking after him. Ever since Rachel had discovered he had only had a potato for his tea, the women had collected food for him amongst themselves, with the result that he lived better now than anyone else on the Mission.

He wasn't sure how to broach the subject. The flies were terrible, and he kept on waving at them while he asked Nerida in a friendly way about her stay in Melbourne. He was in his mid-thirties, his skin was smooth and pink above his black outfit and white collar. He had fair, curly hair. He found it hard to look at her. Indelible in his mind was the scene he had witnessed a short time ago: Nerida, flung back across the desk, and Felton bending over her. If anything, the sight of Felton had been more shocking: his eyes had been glazed, his face had been red and blotched, hair tousled, fly undone, his manliness displayed. He had been reduced to a state of animal passion by this girl . . .

Short felt out of his depth. He was comfortable with women like Ivy, Rachel, and the other ladies attending Bible class. He was truly fond of them: together they would discuss the love of

Jesus and of his heavenly Father, and would dissect appropriate passages in the Good Book. But this . . .

He took another sip of tea, and thought of Jesus and Mary Magdalene. He smiled at Nerida: it must be hard for her after the excitement of the city to get used to the quiet and isolation of a place like Koomalah. He began to talk a lot about temptation and salvation, and the Devil being in all of us and the necessity to grab him by the tail and to throw him out. It took Nerida quite some time to understand what he was leading up to.

'Just a minute! What did Felton say? That I started it?' She was on her feet.

'Let's not level accusations . . .'

She interrupted him, eyes blazing: 'I want to know! If he did, he's lying! I don't throw myself at anyone; least of all Mr Felton!'

She didn't go up to the house after that, but there was no getting away from Felton and his wife. Mrs Felton, on her regular rounds, called in at the Andersons, checked the dusting, the sheets, the blankets. She never looked at Nerida.

She had once more tried to get Felton to resign, and to return with her to Melbourne. He wouldn't hear of it. Where would he find work? No. This job suited him down to the ground. If he had taken up with the women here, she only had herself to blame. She had driven him to it.

He felt he was doing a good job at Koomalah, considering he knew nothing about blacks before. Barely knew that they existed. But here he was, in command of a whole mob of them! His Army training came in handy; he was used to giving orders, to seeing policies implemented. Never questioned them. Why should he? For instance, there was that new scheme: Apprenticeship Training for Young Aboriginal People. It meant taking teenagers from their families and putting them into institutions where the girls were trained as domestics, the boys as station hands. Well, he didn't think much of this scheme: a black would never make a white; they just didn't have it in them. Still, if that's what the policy was, he'd see that it was followed. It was a bit like cattle mustering (not that he knew anything about that, either): you cut the young calves from the rest of the mob, loaded them, and away they went. There was always a big shindy when it happened, but after a while things went back to normal.

This time it was the turn of Alma's two daughters aged twelve and thirteen. Felton was at the store, handing out rations, making sure that Maizie got a bit of extra fat and flour. He gave it to her right in front of Nerida's nose – to show her what she was missing out on. He'd have to deduct it from someone else later on – so what? There were enough who could do with a bit of a lesson.

Then the police car from Quidong arrived and made straight for Alma's house. Good. You had to be quick, to stop the kids from going into hiding. Some had swum the river and hidden in the bush for days. The police were in the house quick as a flash; Alma had barely time to run home from the store with the other women. The kids, screaming and yelling and crying, were put into the car. Alma was sobbing hysterically. Felton and the police were unmoved: the kids would be better off in a Home. Who knows – they might even go up to sunny Queensland!

One of the women had seized a shovel and was ready to attack the constables, but she was disarmed pretty quickly. Felton stood there, unruffled, his baton in his hand, secure.

Then he saw Nerida. She was with her mother. He hadn't seen her coming. She didn't move; she didn't join in the noise, the fracas. She looked at him with such icy contempt and hate that it gave him quite a surprise, quite a shock.

That evening Nerida, Ron, and Andy discussed ways and means of getting rid of Felton. They sat in the kitchen around the table. Grandmother was knitting a jumper for Ron out of old wool. Ivy and Rachel were preparing to visit Mr Short and were putting together some items of food they had collected that day from some of the other women from Bible class. Dad was huddled in his corner next to the stove. He had been getting worse over the last few weeks, and he looked feverish.

Nerida had suggested they get a petition together, to pass on to the Protection Board. None of the older people seemed very keen on the idea, least of all Ivy. The whitefellers would stick together; who'd believe the people at Koomalah would have a just complaint? Anyway, who knew what kind of manager would replace Felton? And it wouldn't stop the kids being taken away; it was the government doing that. Rachel agreed with her.

Nerida had become more and more impatient. 'But he's giving them the names, isn't he? They wouldn't know about the kids if he didn't tell them!'

Ivy shook her head. She was frightened. She felt she could put up with anything as long as her family were safe. The world outside Koomalah was unknown, terrifying, became more threatening every day with the war going on, with the Depression still not over. What if her children were sent off the Mission? The place where they were born? What would happen to them? And there was a rumour that soon Aboriginal people would be declared Australian citizens. They'd be given some kind of certificate – if the manager recommended it. It would entitle them to all sorts of things. 'Yes,' Ron said, 'like going into the pub and get drunk.'

Ivy was sure there would be other things with it than that. If they upset Felton, and if they didn't get him replaced – what then? They'd miss out on their citizenship papers, wouldn't they?

'Piece of paper doesn't give you dignity, Mum', Ron said despairingly.

'That's right!' Nerida looked at her father who was coughing again. 'Look at Dad! He fought at Gallipoli and in France, but do they think of him as Australian citizen? To them he's just an Abo! Who wants their citizenship – if someone like Felton's going to give it to you!'

'Nerida's right. I'm not going to lick their boots for it.' Ron was as exasperated as Nerida. He had found out that Felton had sold some of the Mission's machinery to local farmers and pocketed the money. And what about the trust fund for the workers?

Their father had listened after his coughing fit. He wondered how they'd manage to get any signatures on that petition. Who would have the courage to sign?

Andy had been fairly quiet, listening to both sides of the argument. 'I'll take the petition with me on my rounds,' he said now. 'There's a lot of people sick of the conditions.'

Ivy sighed and gave up.

Nerida looked at her. 'Someone's got to tackle Felton, Mum!' she said. She was glad that Andy was on their side.

Grandmother nodded. 'When I was young we'd have got rid of him long ago. Him and that missionary you are feeding . . .'

About a month later – when Mr Watson of the Aboriginal Protection Board was due for his visit – they had been able to collect a number of signatures on a petition, in which it was 'humbly and respectfully requested to have an inquiry into the management at Koomalah.' Many of the people had been afraid to sign. It was one thing to talk about Felton with other koories who felt the same way about him, but it was a very different matter to put your name down on a piece of paper for some official to see it. Who knew what might come of it! The whitefellers were bound to stick together; they had always done so in the past.

Mr Watson arrived in his car which had a fine cover of dust on it; the drought had not yet broken. Faces peered from behind half-open doors and from behind windows. The tracks between the houses were empty, except for some children playing, and dogs meandering about or sleeping in the shade.

Watson pulled up in front of the manager's house; Felton and his wife came out to greet him on the steps, with a lot of smiles and hand-shaking.

Later the bell was rung at the store, signifying that Mr Watson was ready to talk to the inmates of Koomalah. People slowly began to drift towards the small square.

Nerida, Ron, and Andy were among the first to arrive. Not much later Grandmother came, with Ivy and with Rachel. Grandmother looked strong and proud and completely unafraid. Nerida felt a wave of admiration for the old woman who now came to join her and Ron and Andy, while Ivy and Rachel remained in the background. Nerida's father, too, had come. He stood with some of the other men. They all looked tense, and serious, ill at ease.

'Not many here.' Nerida said with a sinking heart.

Andy nodded. 'They're scared. You can't blame them.'

At last Mr Watson briskly came from the manager's house, followed by Felton who looked efficient, dependable, every inch the manager. They had about them the air of men united in a worthy cause. Watson ruffled the hair of a few children who were hanging about, and he smiled at some of the faces he thought he knew. Some smiled back sheepishly; others turned away.

Now Watson climbed onto the small loading ramp next to the store. He was quite a good-looking man, with wavy hair immaculately combed, blue eyes that had an expression of perpetual sincerity, a rather soft, full mouth and a slightly receding chin which he kept thrust forward.

He raised his voice: 'Good afternoon everyone!' and smiled.

There was no response. He realized that few people had assembled, fewer than at other times, and that there was a feeling of expectancy, of tension. He looked briefly at Felton, whose face was expressionless.

'. . . Well, I've just had a conversation with your manager, and it seems you are all very happy here at Koomalah . . .'

Andy now stepped forward. He was nervous, and for a moment it seemed he had lost his voice. He cleared his throat, took an envelope from his pocket. 'Mr Watson . . . I've got something here for you we'd like you to pass on to the Aboriginal Protection Board . . .'

He held out the envelope.

Nerida stood and watched, fists clenched tightly, her heart in her mouth. Watson once more looked at Felton who seemed puzzled, suspicious and uneasy. A short time ago Watson had asked him if there were any signs of unrest at Koomalah, as there were on the other Missions. Felton had assured him there were not. What the hell was happening?

Felton shot a quick glance at Eddie and Peter, but they apparently didn't know what this was all about either. Then his eyes went to Nerida and Ron who stood behind Andy. It was obvious they were in this together. For a brief moment he remembered how she had looked at him when Alma's girls had been taken away by the police.

Watson accepted the envelope from Andy and stood as if he didn't quite know what to do with it. 'What's your name?' he asked in a friendly but condescending manner.

Now that the envelope had been passed on, Andy regained confidence and self-assurance. What would be, would be; things would take their course. 'Andrew Turner,' he said, and there was a ring to his voice.

Nerida felt proud of him.

'Well,' Watson said, 'is there anything else you want to tell me? Any problems? Or complaints?' He looked at the others, but they were silent.

'You'll find it all in the petition,' Andy said, and he stepped back.

'All right, I'll see you get an answer.' Watson put the envelope into his pocket, and it was all over. For the moment, anyway.

Months passed. Winter came, and with it the rain. The chill came in through the chinks in the walls; the roofs leaked. Many people, already weakened with malnutrition, became ill. They had to get through it unaided: the Mission hospital had ceased functioning; the only equipment consisted of some bottles of antiseptic, a few bandages and sticking plaster.

Bill Anderson, Nerida's father, became worse. He refused to see a doctor despite Ivy's pleading. He felt he was beyond help; why should he degrade himself and go begging to get a permit from the manager to see a doctor who could do nothing for him? He was not afraid to die.

One rainy night he haemorrhaged. There was blood everywhere. Nerida had never seen so much blood. Ron ran up to the house, knocked Felton out of bed though it was one in the morning and got him to ring the doctor who lived at Quidong. The doctor refused to come out on such a rainy night: Koomalah Mission was too far.

Ron and Nerida, chaff bags over their heads against the rain, woke up the Reverend Arthur Short. Short was in a dreadful quandary: he was prepared to help, of course, but did they have a permit from the manager to leave the Mission? Without that it was impossible to do anything; he could not take anyone away without permission. Rules were rules.

115

Ron and Nerida went back to Felton's house; they'd do without Short's help. They would ask Felton himself to drive their father to hospital. Felton refused. It could wait till morning; their father would be all right. Ron flared up: if anything happened to their father, if he died, he would hold Felton responsible.

Felton stared at him: 'You threatening me?'

'It's about time someone stood up to you.'

'I'll have you sent off the Mission.'

'I was born here.'

'I don't care where you were born!'

Ron could hardly speak. 'I'll have no whitefeller tell me to come and go.'

For a moment it looked as if Felton was going to strike Ron. Then he suddenly turned and told them to follow him. He walked into the office. Here was a way to stop the Andersons causing trouble. Ever since the petition had been handed over four months ago he had been worried about a possible inquiry.

He told Ron and Nerida to shut the door. They did. When they came to his desk, he took his army revolver from the drawer, then slowly, deliberately, placed it beside the blotter.

They stared at it, almost in disbelief.

Felton took a small notebook from the desk. 'I've got your name in here, Anderson,' he said, 'along with a few others. I know you're out to make trouble here . . .'

Ron said nothing.

Felton looked at him. 'I could shoot you, and say it was self-defence.' A brief nod towards Nerida. 'Would be her word against mine . . .'

Nerida was close to breaking down. 'Mr Felton, all we ask is that you take my father to hospital, that's all! Will you do it, please!'

'All right, I'll take him –' Felton was very quiet – '*after* your brother has signed a document that he won't cause any more trouble. And you, too. You sign it, too.'

They signed. There was nothing else they could do.

They wrapped Bill Anderson in blankets and waited on the verandah. Ivy was going along; she put on her hat, got her bag.

At last the lights of the Mission truck appeared; then the truck itself lumbered up through puddles and driving rain. It pulled up. Ivy ran to the other side of it to open the cabin door, but Felton pulled it shut. They looked up at him. He got out on his side. 'You and Bill ride in the back,' he said, and started to undo the sideflap of the truck.

'Not in this rain!' Ron couldn't believe his ears.

'No blackfeller rides in the cabin with the manager. You know the rules.' He made to pull himself up, back into the cabin. 'If you don't, learn them now.'

Ron, beside himself with rage, dragged him back down and hit him in the face. Felton reeled and was flung against the truck. Ivy screamed. Nerida grabbed Ron's arm before he could hit again. She was terrified that Felton would now refuse to drive. She was right.

Felton regained his balance. He was oddly, frighteningly calm. 'Right,' he said, 'if that's the way you want it, he can walk.'

Ivy was crying; she was quite inarticulate. She tried to hold on to him, to stop him from getting back into the truck; he shook her off. 'You can thank your son for this.' He turned to Ron. 'I want you off the Mission. Now!'

Lights were going on in the neighbouring houses. Soon there would be a crowd. There could be trouble. Felton was on his own; there were no police around to protect him now. There could be a riot; the mood at Koomalah had not been good in the last few months. He began to feel afraid.

Nerida stepped in front of him. She seemed oblivious to the rain; she did not care about what had happened. Only one thing mattered now: 'Please help Dad, Mr Felton.'

He didn't know what to do without losing face.

Ivy was still crying. Bill Anderson waited, motionless in the rain, the blanket around him like a cape. In the background, barely visible, Grandmother stood in the shadow. She was silent, but he could feel her eyes on him – like a malevolent ghost's.

Felton climbed into the cabin, slammed the door shut. 'All right,' he said abruptly, 'you come along. The rest of you stays here.' He stabbed a finger in Ron's direction.' 'When I come back, I want you gone. If you're still here, watch out.'

They helped Bill Anderson up on the truck. In the back was an empty fruit-case; they put it against the back of the cabin, and he sat on it, barely conscious. As the truck took off, Nerida supported him as best she could.

At last they reached the District Hospital. They were both drenched to the skin, and cold.

Half an hour later Bill was in one of the beds, warm and dry. Here they treated him like a human being. It was what was due to him, but to Nerida it was like a miracle.

She and Felton were given hot cups of tea. After that there was nothing more to be done except go back to the Mission.

Perhaps the attitude at the hospital had had some effect on Felton: he offered that Nerida ride with him in the cabin. She hesitated, but she was cold, exhausted, and he sounded almost human for a change – as if he regretted how callous he had been. Perhaps he hadn't realized how close to death her father was. She accepted.

For a while the truck drove on, and neither of them spoke. He slipped out of his jacket, pushed it towards her. She didn't want it. He insisted. 'Take it,' he said. 'Go on, don't be a fool.' So she put it around her shoulders. It was still warm from his body.

The rain was still pelting down; the wipers on the windscreen could hardly cope. The lights of the truck were weak, and it was difficult to see the road. For a while there was no other sound except that of the engine, the swishing of the wipers, the hissing of the rain. They were cut off from the world in the small cabin of the truck rumbling through the night.

He looked across at her. The light from the panel faintly lit up her face. She looked mysterious, vulnerable, and unreachable. He was drawn to her, fascinated, but his mind could not cope; he could not understand what he felt. He stretched out his hand to touch her.

She cringed. Her eyes were huge and dark as she stared at him, jerked out of her drifting thoughts.

'You are a very pretty girl,' he said.

She moved away from him as far as she could, right against the door, and took the jacket from her shoulders, appalled that he could have misunderstood her reasons for accepting it.

'Please, leave me alone,' she said.

'Oh, come on.' He pulled up. He did not imagine for a moment that she might find him repulsive, undesirable. He stretched out his hand once more to pull her towards him.

'No!' She opened the door to get out. He was exasperated. He didn't mean to harm her. After what had happened she should have been glad he was still willing to take up with her. 'What's with you bloody blacks! I'm buggered if I understand you lot!'

She had got out and stood in the rain, her face distorted with rage and with despair. 'No, you don't, do you? Have you ever thought we're human? Why don't you use your head for once, instead of what's hanging beneath your belt!'

She slammed the door shut, and he saw her disappear into the night. For a moment he didn't know what to do. He wanted to punish her. He wound down the window, yelled her name, but there was no reply. He felt rejected, hurt, and he was furious. 'It's a long walk,' he shouted. Then he pushed the truck into gear and drove off. But there was no satisfaction in what he did: she was beyond his reach.

Nerida watched the truck move off. She stepped back onto the road and began to walk. For quite some time she could see the headlights because the road was so straight, the land so flat. Then the lights vanished, and it was utterly, completely dark. She had to follow the road by feeling the gravel surface with her feet, and now and then she strayed into the grassy edge.

Gradually she got used to the direction of the road. She remembered how she had walked here some months ago. It had been hot and dry and sunny. What had she achieved in that time? What was the meaning of her life? Why was she ever born?

She thought of her father. He had smiled so oddly when she had said goodbye at the hospital – his dark face on the white pillow, haggard, worn, his hair going grey. It struck her how little she knew of him, of his thoughts. He must have thought that this hospital, with its polished floor, its smell of disinfectant, was the last place he would see on earth. He who loved the bush, the open space . . . She thought of the life he should have led. He was in his early fifties; there should have been many good years ahead of him . . .

She began to think of her family, and of all the others who lived at Koomalah, and of those on the other Missions – people she had never seen. She was suddenly filled with a great love for them, and it seemed to her that she understood them clearly; she could see how their needs, their hopes were the same as hers. She felt a deep, almost painful pride in being part of them, in being one with this devastated land.

The rain was much lighter now, and in the east there was a hint of grey. Nerida walked along, a tiny speck under the huge sky. She felt surrounded by some great benevolent power, something that connected her with the vast space around her, something that reached beyond the clouds, and the stars behind them. It was as if her spirit walked through time. A shiver ran through her entire body: not of fear, but of awe. As long as she lived she would never forget that walk along the road to Koomalah.

It was daylight when she got back to the Mission.

Grandmother had taken charge. She looked after Ivy who was still distressed, but relieved that Bill was in good hands, Nerida back home safe. Mr Short turned up, wondering if he could be of help, could do something. 'I think you've done enough already,' Grandmother said and shut the door in his face.

Ron had gone into hiding on the Mission. Nerida went to see him as soon as it was dark again. She remembered the old shack at the edge of Koomalah. They had played there – she and Ron and Andy and some others – when they had been children. It was close to a patch of trees which somehow had been spared when everything else had been cleared for pasture.

She had to go to Ron by a roundabout way, making sure she wasn't seen by Felton's spies or their friends. She brought him some food, and they sat together in the dark, wondering what to do, what the future held. She had talked to Andy in the afternoon, and they had both agreed it was time for the koories at Koomalah to make a stand. They would have to have the courage to give evidence against Felton at the inquiry. Ron was anxious to be involved, but he could not afford to be seen for fear of Felton having him arrested. What good would he be to anyone in gaol?

From that day on Nerida and Andy spent much time visiting the others and telling them how those on other Government Missions had begun to speak out against the way they had to live. It was important to be heard; there was no one else in the country being treated in such a humiliating way. Whitefellers had taken away the land, they had tried to kill the spirit and the culture of the people, and now they hoped that those who remained would quietly fade away. If they did not act now, the gubbahs might succeed. Many whitefellers not involved with Aboriginal affairs did not even know what was going on; there was a conspiracy of silence. They owed it to their children, to their children's children; they owed it to the generations that had gone before – to those who had been massacred, to those whose spirit had been subjugated by the missionaries and by men like Felton – to stand up and be heard and demand their rights to be treated like human beings, like Australian citizens in a land that belonged to them, not like inmates of a penal settlement.

One night the police turned up and searched the Anderson house. They barged into the bedrooms in the middle of the night looking for Ron; they had heard that he was still somewhere on the Mission.

'We don't know where he's gone,' Grandmother said, 'and if we did you'd be the last ones we'd tell.'

The sergeant warned them: 'We'll be back, and if we catch him in this house you'll be charged with harbouring a criminal.'

A few days later Mrs Felton went to Quidong with Mr Short. She ran into the matron of the hospital and by accident found out that Nerida had been with Felton when Bill Anderson had been admitted, and not Ivy – as Felton had maintained.

She had already toyed with the idea of leaving Felton. Now the time had come. This was the final straw.

On the way back she sat in silence in the car. She felt oddly peaceful now. This was it. The dice had fallen. No more inspection tours, no more rows with Felton, no more nothing. She didn't tell Mr Short, but when he dropped her off at her home she said goodbye to him with such dignified finality that he felt something was afoot. He admired her. Admired the way she coped at Koomalah. What strength! What fortitude!

When she got into the house she immediately phoned for a taxi. Then she packed her things. She did not yet know how she would support herself, but she didn't care. Anything was better than being here, with the flies, with Felton, with the blacks. She felt free already and she wondered why she had waited so long to take this final step.

When Felton came into the kitchen for his tea, he found her putting on her hat. Her cases, packed, stood side by side next to the door. She told him his meal was in the oven. She had done her duty to the last; no one could accuse her of neglecting it.

At first he could not understand what was going on, then he felt a twinge of panic. She mustn't leave! He needed her! She was sarcastic and quite calm: Yes, there was an inquiry coming up; let Maizie or Nerida help him out.

Outside the taxi had arrived; some children stood about, wondering what the strange car was doing here.

Mrs Felton went to pick up her cases. Felton barred her way. He assured her that Nerida was a stupid bitch. He didn't care for her; he hadn't touched her – not since the incident in the office. Mrs Felton remained totally unmoved. She didn't care what he did or thought, not any more.

He picked up her cases, trying to hold onto her by holding onto them, but she wrenched them free; and then the taxi driver was at the door, peering in through the fly screen, so he let go.

He watched her from the window as she got into the car after she had made sure the cases had been stored properly in the boot. The taxi drove away, and he was alone.

He got himself a beer and sat down in the kitchen. It was getting dark, but he didn't turn on the light. He had not expected this feeling of emptiness, of deprivation. Somehow Joan had given him a sense of security; she had been like a mother almost. He would rant and rave at her, abuse her, but she had been there, strong, reliable, and solid.

Now he suddenly felt inadequate. He began to think that he should never have left the Army, forgetting that he had been discharged. He was a plain and simple man; why should he have to bother with the blacks in this godforsaken place? He was aggrieved; he had been persuaded to take on this job. He blamed Joan for it. She was responsible, and now she had walked out. She had supported him for a year when he had been unemployed; to please her he had applied, never thinking he'd have a chance. After all, he had never done this kind of thing before; had never bothered about Abos, had never really wanted the bloody job. He smashed the empty glass against the wall and got himself another bottle.

Next morning he told Maizie to move into the house.

He'd never done much on the Mission; now he stopped even pretending. He spent most of his time lazing about, drinking, sleeping, having sex when he could manage. Practically his only contact with the people was through Eddie and Peter. They reported what was going on, often inventing things to extract more booze from Felton. He wondered about Nerida. What was she doing? What had she been up to lately? He vaguely blamed her for his situation; it was because of her that Joan had left. He dreamt up ways of humiliating her, showing her who was boss. But he somehow never put these plans into action. One day he would. One day he'd bring her to her knees.

Nerida, Ron, and Andy decided it was time to act. There still was no word from the Aboriginal Protection Board. It was obvious they had to attract attention in another way: by defying the authorities.

They would organize a meeting at the hall. They would call it without asking for a permit. Ron would be there. He was bound to be arrested: the police had come looking for him several times; this time they'd have no trouble finding him. There would have to be a hearing in a court; the world outside would at last hear what was going on at Koomalah.

The church hall was like every other building in the place: shabby and dilapidated. Andy and Nerida were there early, putting rickety chairs and benches in position, and a table on the platform, with three chairs behind it.

Mr Short appeared on the scene. He was flustered, worried, when he found out what was going on. Did they have permission? Were they aware of the likely consequences of their action? He was appalled when he found out that Andy, the future parson, was one of those responsible for the disobedience. 'You should not be involved! It's not the church's work! It's political!' he said, getting in the way. 'What will the bishop say?'

Andy remained unruffled. 'He might agree with us ...'

Nerida smiled. She and Andy had grown fond of each other.

Later she went to fetch her brother. How things had changed since they had passed around the petition! Over the last fortnight she had tried to touch a chord in the people here, and she felt that she had been able to open their minds to something bigger than themselves. Tonight would be the test to show if she had succeeded. As she hurried to Ron's hide-away she met people going to the hall. Many were dressed in their best clothes, aware of the importance, the significance, of their action. Nerida began to feel that she was part of some great tide, a tide that would carry with it a change for the people everywhere. She was taking part in history.

Ron was waiting impatiently. The last fortnight had been tough on him: he had been condemned to inactivity. He had slept most of the day, and walked about at night. He had done a lot of thinking.

As they left the shack, a chorus of kookaburras started to cackle their defiant laughter.

By the time they arrived at the hall, it was quite dark. The place was lit up by numerous hurricane lanterns, kerosine lamps and candles which the people had brought along. It gave the place a festive look. Peter and Eddie had turned up. They were worried: what would Felton say about them not finding out about this meeting? They would have to say that they had reported it, and that he had forgotten. He might believe it if he was drunk enough.

In their own anxiety, they were warning the others of the dire consequences of the meeting, but they were met with a good deal of sarcasm and biting humour. Grandmother offered to get them some skirts; they were behaving like old women. Others told them to crawl back to where they came from. There was laughter, and an air of defiance.

When Ron entered with Nerida, there was clapping. Grandmother's and Ivy's faces shone with pride: Ron was risking a good deal, and they knew it. They would not let him down. No one would.

He, Andy, and Nerida sat down at the table. They had made some notes. None of them was used to public speaking, but here they were among friends. Ron cleared his throat; he was very moved. He thanked everyone for being here, and he told them that out of this meeting changes would come. Not only for Koomalah, but for the people everywhere.

In the background Mr Short hovered about uneasily, frequently peering through the door, wondering when Felton would hear what was going on, and also whether, perhaps, it was his duty to inform him.

Peter and Eddie had already relieved him of this task. Once the meeting had begun, they had sneaked from the hall and run to Felton's house.

Felton rang the police. While he was waiting for them to arrive, he walked out onto the verandah and stood there, by himself. He felt a coup was being plotted against him, and for a moment or two it was as if he were caught in quicksand. Maizie must have known about the meeting; why didn't she mention it? The ungrateful bitch. He looked at the rows of houses. Most of them were dark, only a few were lit.

There was no doubt in his mind that the Andersons were behind it all. He was filled with a sullen hate when he thought of them. They were ruining his life. He would get even with the whole lot of them, especially Nerida.

At the hall the meeting was going well. Nerida had started shyly and uncertainly, knowing that in the audience there were many who were older, who might not like to be preached at by a young woman like herself. But then she saw that they all listened attentively, without resentment, and she gained courage. It was a new experience for everyone. Once more she talked about the situation on other Missions, the neglect and lack of interest on the part of the authorities, the affrontery that they, who were here long before the whitefellers had come, were denied the basic rights of citizens. 'There's a recruiting poster at the store,' she said. 'It's all right for our men to go and fight in the war, but they've got no say who runs the country! We want the right to vote!'

There were claps and cries of approval.

Nerida felt strong now, and the words came easily. 'There's no one in the country treated in such a humiliating way. We need a permit to get on and off the Mission; we need a permit to see our relatives, or the doctor! Our children are taken away from us and are trained as domestics. I know of one young girl whose mistress hosed her down with cold water for punishment! That girl was thirteen, and there was no one there to help her get away. Where's the future in being trained as servants? What we need is training in agriculture and administration, and school-teaching – so that we can take on more responsibility!'

She was anxious to say as much as possible before the inevitable interruption when Felton would arrive. 'They want us to keep away from our relations who are tribal people. They won't let us speak our language. We'll lose our culture! Our endowments are controlled by the manager; he tells us where we must buy our rations; instead of butter we get rancid fat, and the flour's full of weevils –'

The door was pushed open; Short hastily stepped aside. Felton strode into the hall, accompanied by two constables, big, burly men, prepared for violence. Everybody turned to look at them, and for a brief moment there was complete and utter silence. Nobody in the audience moved.

'Who gave you permission to hold this meeting?' Felton said, his eyes scanning the faces in front of him. He noticed Short, and Short hastily shook his head. Felton pointed at Ron and turned to the constables: 'There's Anderson. That's the man you're looking for.'

Nerida watched the police come towards them. She had known that this would happen, but now that imagination had become reality, she was filled with sudden panic. She cast a quick glance at Ron, whose face was tense and set. She hoped he would submit quietly: Felton and the police would only be too happy for an excuse to beat him up. Andy was very still. She would not have been surprised if he was praying.

The faces in the hall had become a blur, but then she caught the eye of her grandmother. It was clear the old woman knew how Nerida felt, and she was determined to give her courage. A current of strength seemed to radiate from her.

'Right, you're all under arrest,' the constable said, and snapped a pair of handcuffs around Ron's wrists. The other did the same to Andy.

'What's the charge?' Nerida heard herself ask, and she was surprised how calm her voice sounded.

'Holding a meeting without a permit,' the constable said. Then he looked at Ron: 'Being an unauthorized person on the Mission, and assault.'

They were bustled down the aisle amidst cries of anger, indignation. Rachel was weeping. Ivy sat as if frozen, her eyes wide and full of fear.

Felton had remained near the door. 'I'm going to have you charged with treason,' he said smugly, gloatingly, 'and I'm going to make it stick.' He had read about it in the papers: the country was at war, and anyone enticing others to riot, to rebel against the government, was laying himself open to be accused of treason, of subversion. He'd teach the Andersons and all the others a lesson they would not forget.

Nerida, Ron, and Andy had at first been shaken by the seriousness of the charge. But then they realized there could be some advantages: the case – if they were committed for trial – would be heard in the Supreme Court in Melbourne. There was a good chance the big newspapers would report proceedings, and many people here and overseas would learn about conditions at Koomalah and the treatment of koories there and on other Government Missions. It made everything they had to go through worthwhile; it made the squalor and degradation of the lock-up bearable; even the possibility of a long prison sentence could be faced with fortitude.

The magistrate on his country rounds arrived at last at Quindong. He was anxious to return to Melbourne; he did not like the country much. He quickly dealt with a charge of 'wilful damage', another of 'assault'. Then Nerida, Ron, and Andy were in the dock.

Ivy was there, and Rachel, and Grandmother. Mr Reilly had driven them from Koomalah. The three women sat with him, wearing their best clothes and their hats, handbags on their laps. Ivy and Rachel were tense and worried, Grandmother grim and proud. The magistrate was a small, balding man with a thin moustache. He had no particular feelings about Aborigines. He prided himself on being fair, on never differentiating between white and black when they stood before him.

When he learnt that the three accused were charged with treason he was nettled. He had never had to deal with anything of that kind, and he wished the Prosecution had not brought it up. He stared at the papers, then peered at the accused. 'This is a very serious charge,' he said. He turned to the sergeant who was waiting impatiently. 'Are you sure this is the right court for it?'

'Yes, Your Worship.'

The magistrate sighed resignedly. 'Then let's get on with it ...' He did not have much faith in the sergeant's judgement, considering him an uneducated country yokel, but it seemed best to proceed, and to get the whole thing over and done with as quickly as possible.

He looked once more at the three in the dock. Did they know they were entitled to legal representation? Yes, they did. They wanted to ask their own questions, conduct their own case. The sergeant testily pointed out the presence of Mr Watson; he was here on the prisoners' behalf. Nerida wondered whose side he would really be on.

The hearing started. Nerida, Ron, and Andy sat, tense in anticipation for the moment when they could ask their questions.

Felton was in the witness box. He looked unusually suave, every inch the manager. Nerida wished the magistrate could see him as he normally was, but there was no chance of that. Felton stated that there never had been any insubordination on the Mission under his management until Nerida returned to her family. He was convinced that outside influences were at work, that she had come back with the intention of inciting violence and unrest. Nerida was staggered; so were the other two. Felton brought forth all these accusations with the air of a completely concerned, trustworthy citizen.

The magistrate wondered if he had any evidence to support this claim. No, he had not. He also had to admit that now and then there had been a bit of trouble on the Mission.

Nerida noticed that the magistrate was not a stupid man, that he did not believe everything that Felton said. When Felton pointed Ron out as one of the trouble-makers and stirrers on the Mission, the magistrate wanted to know about the circumstances that led to the assault.

Nerida, Ron, and Andy felt a surge of hope. But the sergeant rose and hastily declared that the assault and the circumstances leading up to it were irrelevant to the charge.

Ron leapt to his feet: 'He made my father sit on the back of the truck in the pouring rain when he was sick!'

He was told not interrupt. If he did not hold his tongue, he would be up for contempt of court.

Ron could not understand. How could something of such importance be irrelevant? What kind of justice could they expect? He was filled with futile rage.

Andy was more fortunate. He quietly managed to establish that Felton hardly ever gave permission to hold meetings, and that there had been no hope at all of his allowing the one in question. He also brought up the subject of the Trust account of which no one had ever seen a penny; but he could go no further because this, too, was considered irrelevant.

There seemed no chance of explaining anything that mattered. Whatever they hoped to bring to public notice was brushed aside as irrelevant. Nerida felt hopeless and frustrated. After all the planning, after all the excitement, this! Andy, too, was despondent, bitter. Ron sat, fists clenched, ready to explode. Nerida prayed he wouldn't: it would only make matters worse.

Then Mr Short entered the witness box. They had almost forgotten about him. Mr Short, having been called as a witness for the Prosecution, gave the sergeant a surprise. 'I have prayed for guidance,' he said softly, 'and I do not think these young people quite realized the gravity of their misdemeanour as far as the unauthorized meeting was concerned. I am certain they are quite genuine in their desire to help their people.'

The sergeant's face was sour. He would have liked to cross-examine Short as a hostile witness, but the magistrate ruled against it. Andy and Nerida felt a faint glimmer of hope. Could it be that Mr Short was willing to speak out? Nerida asked permission to put a few questions to Mr Short: could he describe to the magistrate the conditions at Koomalah . . .?

Short faltered. He was not prepared for this. He saw Felton sitting there, looking grim. '. . . Well,' he said, 'conditions are pretty hard, of course, but they are hard everywhere . . .' He cleared his throat,' To be truthful, I suggest the people at Koomalah are not too badly off . . .'

Nerida and the others did not believe their ears.

Short continued. He had found, he thought, an opportunity to show the magistrate how kind the natives really were. 'I remember with gratitude how Mrs Anderson and Mrs Turner who are both here in court today provided me with evening meals better than some of our white brethren have seen for years . . .'

Nerida looked at her mother, but she could not see her face which was turned towards Short. Oh, Mr Short – could he ever understand?

The magistrate was anxious to conclude the case. He was nettled that he had to waste his time; he blamed the sergeant for it, and made no secret of his feelings. It was obviously a matter that had to be dealt with by the Protection Board. He turned to Mr Watson who had not said a thing, and was assured that an inquiry would be held in the not too distant future.

Then he testily dismissed the charge of treason, and, expressing concern about the rebellious spirit of the three before him, put them on a six-months good-behaviour bond.

They were stunned. Case dismissed! A good-behaviour bond! They had been treated like naughty children who had made a nuisance of themselves. Grandmother, Ivy, and Rachel were relieved: it had been terrible to see their children handcuffed like common criminals.

They stood outside the court not sure what to do next, where to go from here. The only one who was pleased was Mr Reilly, who considered the magistrate a 'true white man' who had seen through the likes of Felton. There was no point in trying to explain, so they let it be.

Felton marched past, with Short, but they did not look across. They got into Short's car and drove off.

Ivy and the others then decided to visit Bill Anderson in hospital, but visiting hours were over, and they were not allowed to see him. So they returned to Koomalah.

Felton had agreed that Ron could collect his things, but that was all. He wanted him off the Mission, and Mr Watson could understand his reasons. So Ron and Andy decided to try their luck in Melbourne. They left the following day.

Life dragged on at Koomalah. There was no purpose. The people who had been roused by expectation of some change once again lost hope, became more lethargic than before. Nerida felt as if they were all locked in a box. There were holes so that they could look out, but the whitefellers had the key, and the people could not get their hands on it. They were locked in the box forever.

Nerida's father died. The curlew, the bird of death, brought them the message, so that they knew long before the hospital rang the manager and asked him to pass on the news. They sat together in the dark, and the moon was very bright outside, and everything was cold and still. Three times the call came, each time a little fainter as the bird flew away. 'He's out of his suffering,' Grandmother said at last.

A few days later the body was brought back for burial at the Koomalah cemetery.

Short conducted the funeral service. He was uneasy; he realized he had done something to upset this family, but he was not sure what it was. After all, he had spoken of their kindness; he felt it was largely thanks to him that they had got off so lightly. He despaired of ever understanding any of the blacks.

While his voice babbled gently and evenly, like running water, Nerida stood barely listening. Her eyes were fixed on the simple coffin in which her father lay. Soon his body would return to the earth from which he had come. From which they all had come. The earth had been his flesh, his blood, his sinews.

She raised her eyes and looked at those assembled around the grave. Many were crying bitterly. It was a bleak and windy day, and leaves were blowing aimlessly through the air. Grandmother had been right when she had said he was better now in the place where he had gone: his spirit home. There his spirit could run free. Till he was born again.... Born to what? Into what kind of world?

And then she noticed two men approaching between the graves. They were in uniform. She realized with a shock they were Ron and Andy. They had joined the Army!

Ron looked at her, then silently took his place next to her and her mother. Andy stood next to Rachel.

Nerida wondered what her father would have thought if he had seen Ron now. 'Let them fight their own wars,' Ron had said not that long ago, just after Nerida had arrived at Koomalah.

Later, when they were seated in the tiny kitchen, he said bitterly that he and Andy had joined to 'fight for the freedom of this country'. The moment he and Andy had arrived in Melbourne, the police had been hounding them. Joining the Army seemed the only solution to get away from them.

They had brought some presents – very practical: lamb chops, sugar, butter. Once again Nerida realized how good it was to be with people she could trust. She began to talk about leaving Koomalah and, to her surprise, her mother agreed with her. With Bill dead and Ron in the Army, there was nothing now to hold her back. Grandmother, too, thought it was best. She would leave, too – despite her age. Even Rachel began to feel it was the only thing worth doing.

Ron and Andy did not agree. They would be earning, they would send money; things might improve at Koomalah once the inquiry was held. If the women left, the police would be after them; the government would force them to return. Nerida did not argue. She did appreciate that Ron and Andy were worried that they might find life outside the Mission worse than they could imagine. But what could be worse than the slow death of one's spirit? It was far better to live in a tent, a humpy, and be free, than to stay at Koomalah where nothing would ever change. She remembered how she had left Felton and the shelter of the truck, and had walked through the darkness and the rain. It had been the right thing to do: things had begun to happen after that.

A fortnight later Felton received a letter from the Protection Board stating the date of the inquiry. He was standing in the middle of his office, which hadn't been cleaned for weeks. He scratched his neck: he'd have to get his books together one of these days...

Then he walked back into the kitchen where Maizie was playing records on the gramophone. He poured himself a beer, and had another look at the letter.

Someone was ringing the bell at the bottom of the stairs. Neither he nor Maizie moved to answer it. It rang again; then he heard someone calling him. He went to see who it was.

Peter and Eddie were almost dancing with excitement: 'There's something going on. Come and have a look, Mr Felton ...'

Maizie, by now very much in charge, waved a hand: 'Go away. Mr Felton's busy.'

Peter and Eddie looked up at the couple, and they grinned. The whole situation was a huge joke to them. 'They're all leaving, Mr Felton...' They waited for the news to sink in.

Everywhere on the Mission the people were moving out. There were hand carts, horse carts, bicycles, old cars; everything that had wheels had been put to use for the great walk-out from Koomalah Government Mission.

Reilly's truck was there, too. Ever since he had learnt that Ron had joined the Army he had kept in touch. He was helping to load Ivy's and Grandmother's belongings.

Rachel was leaving with them. She was already seated on the truck, in an old chair, clutching her handbag, and she was the first to see Felton coming from the house.

She told Nerida, but Nerida did not look in his direction. She just went on securing things on the truck. She felt defiant, proud. He could not touch her. Nor the others. He only had power over them as long as they accepted it.

Felton came straight towards the Andersons. There was no doubt in his mind that Nerida was behind all this. As he approached he saw her moving briskly around the truck, her hair blown about by the wind, her eyes bright – and he found that he still wanted her. There was a feeling of freedom about her, of honesty, of resilience and strength.

He planted himself next to the truck: 'Where the hell do you think you're going?'

She did not answer.

'I haven't given you a permit to go anywhere.'

'We're leaving all the same.'

'You're still on a good behaviour bond; I'll ring the police.'

'You do that, Mr Felton.'

She tied the end of the rope which she had flung across the truck. Now Reilly came from the house, followed by Grandmother and Ivy. 'You've got no permit, Ivy; if you and the others leave the Mission you'll never get back on.'

'That's all right by us.'

Felton did not know what to say. He would never have believed that someone like Ivy would defy him.

Reilly helped her and Grandmother into the cabin of the truck.

Felton looked around: a few of the neighbours were looking across briefly, then went on with their packing. Felton turned on Reilly: 'You got no permit, either, to come on the Mission, have you!'

'There's ladies present, or else I'd tell you what you can do with your permits, Felton . . .'

Felton was suddenly filled with panic. He had despised the people, but now he felt abandoned. Without them he would be nobody. Nothing at all. He dreaded the thought of the empty houses; he would be left in a ghost town, in the middle of nowhere.

He barred Nerida's way. 'This is the last time I'm asking you. You ought to be bloody glad I'm still willing to give you a go . . .'

'Get out of my way, Mr Felton.' She looked straight at him, and said very quietly, 'There's no one in the world I despise as much as you.'

She got onto the truck, Reilly behind the wheel. Felton looked around: everywhere the cars and carts had begun to move, accompanied by those who left on foot, and by their dogs. The people barely looked at him as they passed.

Reilly started up the engine.

'You're breaking the law, every one of you!' Felton yelled in a rage. He turned to Peter and to Eddie who had been watching curiously. 'Come on, you two! Get them off the truck!' But they didn't move. They knew a loser when they saw one.

Nerida gave him one last glance. 'Why don't you go and sober up,' she said.

And so the people left Koomalah Government Mission.

L o - A r n a,
the Beautiful

G ranny Johnston spent most of her time sitting in an old rickety armchair outside her humpy on the shanty site. It was more a hut, really; it was better constructed than the others, though it was made of wood and corrugated iron sheets collected from the rubbish tip not far away. It had a small verandah, and a vegetable patch. She'd sit in the chair, in her long, dark frock, her white hair in a neat bun at the back of her head, her walking stick next to her, and often she'd have a copy of the Bible on her lap, open. But she wouldn't read. It was just there for company.

She was like a queen. She had such dignity.

The people at the site, they respected her. They liked to do things for her: they'd get her shopping in the small country town called Kyewong about twenty kilometres along the highway; they'd fetch water for her from the single tap the Council had installed when the place was supposed to be a picnic spot for the whitefellers from the city; they'd dig her vegetable patch and plant her tomatoes and lettuce for her.

And then she'd look at them with her magnificent shining deep black eyes, but she'd never say 'Thank you' or anything like that. She had given up talking a long time ago. Gradually she had said less and less: as the world grew noiser, she grew more silent. And now, while the huge semi-trailers roared past on the highway, planes hummed overhead, bulldozers clanked and heaved as they pushed the soil over the garbage at the tip, and the youngsters listened to their transistors all day long because there was nothing else to do, and there was news of wars and explosions and disasters everywhere, she had stopped talking altogether.

People thought it was because she was old. 'Her mind is drifting,' they said.

But it wasn't that. Her grand-daughter, Alice Wilson, she was sure there was another reason for that silence, though she would never have questioned the old woman about it. She knew that the old people can do many things. Whitefellers think they are the first who ever thought of time travel, but the koories – they have known about it all along. To them time is like an ocean, not a stream.

Granny Johnston, like the elders of the tribal people, could send her mind into another time. She knew what the shanty site had been like hundreds of years ago – when the trees that were there now had been nothing but hard brown seeds. She knew the river which ran close by, knew its source which was still hidden in the mountains. She knew what it had been like when the big fish was resting in its cool clear water, when the women had gathered reeds for baskets, lily roots for food.

In her own lifetime she had seen many things. She had lived on a Government Mission, and she had rebelled, like the others, against the management, and had walked off to live in a humpy near the river. She had known many of those who had fought for a better life for the people. There had been a new feeling in those days – as if the tide was slowly turning.

Still, here she was living on a shanty site, like forty years ago. It was another site, another river, but the conditions were the same. People had come and gone . . . She thought of all those she had known, and who had died. Many had been quite young. Like the girl who had tried so hard to get better schooling for the kids . . . To Granny Johnston all these people were alive. All you had to do was to send your mind out to them into what others called 'the past'.

But there was someone – one small girl – she did not know how to meet. Every time – and it was often – when her thoughts searched for her, they were lost in a void. Her great-granddaughter. Lo-Arna. Alice's little daughter.

A short distance away Alice was washing clothes in an old zinc tub. She and Jimmy Randle and their two sons lived in a caravan here on the site. Soon they'd be leaving. The grape-picking season wasn't far away. She'd miss them, but eventually they'd come back. Though by that time the shanty site might be no longer there. The garbage tip was almost full and the Council was threatening eviction: they wanted the land to subdivide into hobby farms. Perhaps a miracle would take place: they had been promised decent housing a couple of years ago; perhaps she'd live long enough to experience it . . .

It was peaceful here at the shanty site. High above, in the still air, a plane hummed its way to Melbourne. It seemed to belong to another world. The city was about two hours drive away, and you could see the sky in that direction covered with a brownish haze. Granny had been to Melbourne a few times, but she didn't care for the place: it hadn't been much fun breathing that pungent air. She felt sorry for the people who had to have it in their lungs all the time – especially the kids. True, here at the site they had to put up with the stink from the tip when the Council burnt some of the rubbish, but that wasn't very often, and if they were lucky the wind blew in the opposite direction.

Her great-grandson Peter was teaching himself a country-and-western tune on that old guitar of his. He had a small transistor cassette recorder going with the song on it, and he was trying to copy what he heard. He had almost got the hang of it. He had a pleasant voice, and she liked to hear him sing.

She was in a strange mood today – detached, yet part of everything. As she sat there in her chair everything seemed to stand out very clearly – as if etched with a sharp instrument into time.

She looked across at Jimmy who was chopping wood. He had had a lot of practice doing it and it was beautiful to see him: there wasn't a wasted move, and the axe came down with just the right power each time to split the wood cleanly. He wore a green pullover, and she could almost see each stitch in it. There was a hole at his elbow. He was in his early forties, and here and there a grey streak showed in his curly hair. Alice had been lucky meeting him. They had never married, but he was a good husband. He hadn't had much schooling, but he was a thinker. He didn't drink – just a glass of beer now and then. And he loved his family.

That was the most important thing in life: to love each other. In the days when Granny Johnston had still talked now and then, she had told the others that it didn't matter whether you were black, white or brindle, you had to love one another. She hadn't really had too much success with that remark: the people were happy to love other koories, but the whitefellers – how the hell could you love them! And they didn't love you back. Not that you would have wanted their love, anyway.

Still, the feeling of love and trust and affection among the people on the site – that was quite evident. That's what made it possible to live here, despite the rain and the wind and the cold in winter, and the flies and the heat in summer.

Some women were standing at the tap, filling their buckets with water. Not far from them a few men were playing cards. Children used the shell of an old car as a cubby house, and dogs were lying around asleep.

She looked across at Alice who had finished washing and was helping young Jamie with his sums. Alice was in her late thirties. She had a gentle face, but strong. And she kept her figure, unlike many other women of her age who tended to become fat and flabby. Alice wore jeans and a checked blouse, and she moved with the grace of the tribal people. Granny could hear her voice, though she was speaking quietly; Peter had stopped playing and was once more rewinding the tape on his recorder; the plane above had disappeared.

'Four and four, come on, Jamie . . .'

Jamie's eyes were on a beetle that was crossing the wooden table.

'Come on, you want to be a pilot, don't you? So you've got to do your sums . . .'

Jamie surreptitiously counted on his fingers. 'Eight,' he said at last, and there was a note of triumph in his voice.

Alice ruffled Jamie's hair. Granny Johnston felt a wave of affection and compassion as she watched her. Alice didn't speak much of her little girl. She had never told Jimmy that she had a daughter, but Granny Johnston knew that – like herself – she carried the loss of Lo-Arna with her everywhere.

The noise of a car broke into her thoughts. The engine sounded pretty sick, but it chugged along, and finally an old station wagon came into view over the bumps and through the potholes on the track. It was painted bright blue, and it had patches of primer and a lot of dents and scratches. There were stickers galore: 'Land Rights Now!' and 'Leave Uranium in the Ground', and lots of others.

Now she could see Val herself. She was waving with one hand to the people she was passing and steering with the other. She pulled up: she had made it, despite the engine boiling. She got out, slamming the door shut. She was a big woman, and she was fond of bright colours: she looked like a giant rosella in her green and red frock and yellow-striped cardigan. She had a ribbon in her hair. Her hair was shiny and black and beautiful.

She came across to Granny Johnston first of all and gave her a quick kiss. And a hug. 'How are ya, Granny? Good to see you . . .'

Alice and Jimmy came over to welcome her, and Peter left his guitar and the recorder he had borrowed from a mate. 'New model, eh, Auntie?' He had a huge grin on his face. 'Runs on steam . . .'

Val glared at the car. 'Had to pull up about fifty times to put water in,' she said. 'I'm sick of the old heap.'

Peter loved fiddling with cars. He kept the family car on the road – with Jimmy's help. 'Must be the thermostat; what do you reckon, Dad?'

Jimmy thought it could be that and a lot of other things. They'd have a look later on, when things had cooled down a bit.

Alice meanwhile had taken the waterbag from its hook next to the door of the caravan. She was going to make tea.

When they were seated round the table Val gave them her report. She had talked to the bloke in the Housing Commission office, the one who was in charge of Aboriginal housing among other things, and she had tried to get him to name the date when the people would be able to move in to the new homes they had been promised. Well, you just couldn't pin him down. He was a real expert in avoiding a straight answer. Everything depended on things outside his control. That's what he kept on saying, anyway.

The others listened in grim silence. They could hear the bulldozer working on the garbage tip. It was a menacing sort of noise: like a monster that eats up everything in its path. It was a real gubbah tool, relentless and destructive.

Val told them the field workers in the city were planning a demonstration to pressure the man from the Commission. She wanted Alice to come along, Alice and some others from here at Kyewong.

Alice wasn't keen. She didn't like going to the city; she felt like a stranger there. She didn't like politics. She taught Aboriginal culture to the kids; that's what she felt she could do well. She wouldn't know what to say to that government feller . . .

Val looked at her with an odd expression, but didn't push too much. Just pointed out that she should be there. It wasn't only the people at Kyewong who desperately needed roofs over their heads; the ones at Malton were in the same boat. Jimmy, too, thought that Alice should take part, but he left it up to her. No point pushing her into something she felt was wrong for her.

Granny had been watching Val, and she felt that Val was holding back something. She was right. The moment Jimmy and Peter had gone off to see if they could fix Val's car – temporarily at least – she came out with it.

'Have a guess who the bloke is, Alice. The bloke at the Commission . . .'

'Wouldn't have a clue.'

'Doug Cutler.'

The name hung in the air. Alice sat quite still. Somewhere a bird was singing a small silvery tune against the rumbling, clanking, of the dozer.

Val could already see their battle won. 'Just imagine what he'll think when he claps eyes on you! Be a reminder what he did when he was still a little fish . . .'

Alice couldn't think. It was as if she was caught in a whirlpool. When at last she was able to say something, her voice was low and thick: 'I don't want to see him again. Ever. Not after what he's done to me.'

But Val wasn't going to give up. 'It'll give us a nice start on him! A good bargaining position. He'll be scared out of his wits! It's already rocked him when he realized he'd met me before . . .'

'He'd never know who I was! It's twenty years . . .!'

'You haven't changed that much.'

'I couldn't stand the sight of him.' Alice's voice was shaky.

'For goodness sake, we need your help!' Val looked at Granny, hoping for support.

But Granny Johnston was in another world. 'Doug Cutler.' When she had heard these words she felt a moment had come she had long been waiting for. That they all had been waiting for.

It was as if some fog was about to lift. Something that had been incomplete would be made whole . . .

She would not try to persuade Alice. What was to come, would come.

Doug Cutler was Lo-Arna's father.

That night Alice could not sleep. She tossed and turned till Jimmy woke up and grumbled. She forced herself to lie still, but her mind raced in circles. She thought of Cutler, and how she had trusted him. How proud she'd been! What a fool . . . And she thought of Lo-Arna. Lo-Arna, the beautiful: that's what she had called her daughter. She saw her as she was eighteen years ago, learning to talk, coming towards her, arms outstretched, waiting to be picked up and kissed. How lovely she had been! Her heart ached at the thought: her skin a golden brown, the kind whitefellers tried to get by lying in the sun for hours. Her eyes were large and dark and shiny, and full of laughter and of gentleness. She remembered the warmth of the small body against hers when her daughter had snuggled up for protection, love . . . Since Lo-Arna had gone, part of her own spirit had been missing.

What if Doug Cutler asked about Lo-Arna? She didn't think he would – he wouldn't want to remember that he was the father of her baby – but what if he did? She'd have to tell him that Lo-Arna had been taken away by welfare workers as a neglected child. And he would think she had been a bad mother!

Not that she cared what he thought. Yes, she would go to Melbourne. She wouldn't speak to him, but she would make sure he'd see her. She would haunt him, appear like a spectre from the past. Make him share the guilt she felt. Guilt? Why? She had done nothing wrong. Except trust a gubbah . . .

Three car-loads of koories went from Kyewong to the city. Alice was in the corner in the back seat of one of them, very quiet. It was dark by the time they drove over the West Gate Bridge. Alice could see the city stretching out – vast but lonely, as if each one of these millions of lights was sending a twinkling plea for recognition out into the universe. She wondered if, perhaps, her daughter was near one of those lights somewhere . . . Was she even alive? Who knew? She might have died, unwanted and unloved.

The others in the car were keyed up, singing and chattering. They knew that Doug Cutler was guest of honour at the annual dinner of the Ethnic Soccer Association. The function was being held in one of the eastern suburbs. The houses were all very big and new, on large blocks. There was a huge shopping complex with palm trees in front of it; it had a bright orange dome that looked as if it were made of plastic. There were traffic lights and many lanes and signs and arrows everywhere. A large billboard pictured a man sitting on a horse looking satisfied over the caption: 'This is Marlboro Country'.

Alice was staring through the window without seeing anything. The closer they got to their destination, the more she wished she hadn't come. What was the point? The past was past.

They were late. Groups of koories were already there, holding placards and yelling 'We want Cutler! We want Cutler!' A camera crew had just arrived and was getting organized to film an interview with Val Pearce, who waved frantically when she saw Alice to make her come across. Alice shook her head and stayed by the car.

The doorman, a Greek, was worried. He kept on saying 'This is a nice place, you can't come in here!' and he darted anxious glances in the direction from where he hoped the police would soon arrive.

'Go back to your own country!' one of the women yelled.

'I'm as Australian as you are!' the doorman shouted back.

'That'll be the day!' There was defiant laughter.

'One-two-three-four,
chuck him out the front door . . .'

Some of the koories had started chanting. Alice wished she could see through the walls. Cutler must be aware of what was going on outside. If they had got married – as he once had said they would – would she be in there with him now? Probably not. Most likely he himself would not be there. He wouldn't have got as far in his career with an Aboriginal wife.

'He's coming out the back door!' One of the youngsters came running round the corner, and the next moment Alice found herself caught up in the crowd rushing to trap Cutler before he could get away. The cameraman, technicians and interviewer, all tied together by their cables, hurried alongside him.

Alice saw him scuttling through the car park. A woman was with him; she was hampered by her long evening dress, so she hitched up her skirt to run. She looked very scared. Two men had ventured out with them to escort them to their car. They were no heroes either.

Cutler turned and stopped. He must have realized he couldn't get away. Alice got a shock when she saw what the years had done to him. He was pale – like someone who spends a lot of time indoors. When she had known him he had been tanned by sun and wind. His once thick blonde hair had gone thin and he was nearly bald. There were bags under his eyes, and two sharp shadows ran from his nostrils down to the corners of his mouth. But his body was still firm in the smart dinner suit, and under different conditions he might have looked impressive. Here, trapped like a rabbit, he seemed aware of how undignified his position was.

147

Alice could see him talking to Val; he was trying to convey that the whole thing had just been a huge misunderstanding on the part of the Aborigines.

Alice had moved slightly forward, and Cutler briefly caught sight of her as he tried to put one of the hecklers in his place. There was no sign of recognition. But his eyes were drawn back to her, as if they were playing tricks on him. When it struck him that it was really her, she could see him reel as he was assailed by all the implications. He turned back to Val, collected himself, and managed to sound brisk and efficient: 'Well, get these papers to me Monday morning, and I'll see what I can do . . .'

Val was very smug. 'We'll get them to you before that,' she said. 'We want an appointment Monday morning to discuss them with you.'

'Yes, well, ten o'clock. On the dot.'

'Don't worry. We'll be there . . .'

He didn't give Alice another glance, just got into his car, in which his wife was waiting anxiously, and drove off.

Alice wondered what she had seen in him twenty years ago. He had been so free and open in those days – so unlike the other gubbahs. He had been so ready to take on the world with its prejudice and injustice. She wondered if he had really been like that, or had pretended. Or perhaps she had imagined it. Perhaps she had wanted him to be that way. She, in her stupid dreams, her vanity. She was glad now it had all come to nothing.

Two days later she was down by the river with the kids from the shanty site, teaching them the culture. It was still beautiful round here; you could forget that there was a garbage tip not far away. The trees were big and hardy, and their branches and twigs made a delicate pattern against the pale blue sky. The sun was shining on the water, so that you could see golden ripples on the rocks at the river bank. A wagtail sat close by and watched, turning his small body from one side to the other, chattering. Who was his message for?

Alice told the children about the city – the skyscrapers, the concrete everywhere. And she said: 'The earth is sacred whatever you put on top. Wherever you walk, you walk on holy ground. It hasn't changed. It's the people who have changed.

The culture hasn't walked away from the people; it's the people who have walked away from the culture. Don't you ever walk away. Don't walk away from the meaning of life . . .'

Val Pearce was coming towards them on the narrow path between the trees. Alice told one of the older boys to show the others how to make tracks in the dirt with your fingers – tracks like a lizard's or a dingo's – then she went to meet Val to see if she'd been successful at her meeting with Doug Cutler.

'I've got some news,' Val said. She was grave. Then her voice was gentle: 'I think I've found your daughter.'

Alice stood and stared at her. For a few moments she felt incapable of doing or understanding anything. Then her knees buckled under her and she sat down.

'Cutler's got her.' Val sat down next to her, and put her hand on Alice's arm. 'I saw her at his house. When I took him the documents.'

Alice leant forward and buried her face in her hands, trying to calm the storm that was inside her.

'She's your daughter. She looks very much like you, but she's quite fair. And she calls him "Dad" . . .'

Alice could only whisper: 'Did you . . . speak to her?'

'Not much. Cutler made sure of that. Sent her away quick smart. They had a party going.'

And then it struck Alice: it must have been Doug who had sent those social workers! He who took her child away from her! It was he who had caused all the misery, the heartbreak, she had been through!

'I want to see her.' She was close to tears. 'I want to see my daughter . . .'

Val put an arm around her. 'Alice,' she said gently, 'I think you ought to know that she's got no idea she's Aboriginal . . .'

Alice didn't answer. She knew what Val implied, but what did it matter? Her daughter was alive!

Lo-Arna was in her room on the first floor of the split-level home in a street lined with liquidambar trees. She believed she was Ann Cutler.

She had just got home from university, and thought it would be nice to have a quick dip in the pool in the back garden. She put on her swimsuit and was just about to leave the room when she caught sight of herself in the mirror.

She studied her reflection. Ever since Sunday afternoon, off and on, she had done the same: she had studied her appearance critically, anxiously, and with puzzlement. She could still hear the woman's voice: 'I've seen you before somewhere, haven't I? You're Aboriginal, aren't you?' Why would anyone think that? Not that she believed for a moment there was any truth in it, but the idea that someone could suspect it worried her. She knew little about Aborigines. A picture sprang to mind of some of them seated in the river-beds around Alice Springs, covered in flies, of children with mangy dogs. Now and then her father talked of their drinking problems. On the whole they were a group one seldom talked about, although from discussions at uni, she knew they struggled for land rights.

Her reflection looked back at her: slim, a smooth fair skin with a golden-brown tinge to it. Her eyes were large and dark and showed very little white, her lips were full but delicate, her wavy hair was black. She picked up a hand-mirror and looked at her profile. No, there was no sign of heavy brows, of a broad fleshy nose, of the looks she associated with the blacks. She was relieved. The woman must have tried to be friendly. Wanted to ingratiate herself, perhaps. Or perhaps wanted to upset her: her father had said she was a trouble-maker.

She picked up her towel and went confidently downstairs: she was French Polynesian, and she was an idiot to be upset by a stupid incident like that.

Joy Cutler was in the kitchen, trying out a new recipe – something that had a lot of exotic spices.

For a moment Lo-Arna thought she might tell Joy about the funny incident after all, just for a laugh. But she changed her mind – she didn't quite know why. Perhaps because Joy might have fretted, or got nettled. She had found that Joy, for some reason or the other, didn't like talking about the adoption. She couldn't understand why Ann was always trying to find out details of her background. Why did she worry? She was a Cutler now, that was all that mattered.

Lo-Arna dived into the pool and swam a few lengths, savouring the cool, clean water around her body. She turned and floated on her back, and looked up into the blue sky with its few white clouds. Her mind began to drift, and an image came to her, something that she had seen now and then over the years when she had just been ready to drop off to sleep: a face was bending over her, and the woman's hair was like the clouds. The face was dark and in shadow, but she could see the eyes which were like her own. It was so faint a memory, she could not relate it to anything, but it was pleasant, soothing, comforting. Who could the woman be? Her grandmother, perhaps; some old Polynesian woman . . .?

Alice was driving along the mainstreet of Kyewong. She had told Jimmy she had to do some shopping. He looked at her a little oddly: she must have sounded strange. She hated hiding things from him, but at the moment she could not go into lengthy explanations. He just had to wait.

She was going to ring Doug Cutler. She dreaded the thought of it, of having to get past all those receptionists and secretaries he must have in his office, but she would go through with it.

She made herself step into the phone booth, and she dialled the number Val had written down for her on a piece of paper. She forced herself to concentrate, to put the right number of coins into the slot, to have more ready in case she had to wait.

A woman answered. Alice's own voice sounded strange to her as she gave the name: 'Doug Cutler'.

'I'll see if he's available . . . Who's speaking, please?'

'Alice Wilson.'

She waited. An eternity . . .

'He's in conference at the moment.' The secretary was glib, efficient. How many times had she told that lie? 'Can I take a message?'

Alice hung up and left the booth. 'What message?' she thought bitterly.

Next day, after Alice had been down by the river with the children, there was a telegram for her. Jimmy handed it to her; he had opened it. It said: 'Meet me at the Royal Oaks 8.30 tonight. Need to discuss things with you. Doug Cutler.'

Alice stared at the message, and she could feel Jimmy watching her.

'What does that bloke want?' he said at last. He sounded puzzled and suspicious.

She didn't look at him. 'Must be about the housing . . .'

She wished now she had told Jimmy about Lo-Arna long ago. Why had she been so secretive?

'Why doesn't he come here?' Jimmy asked.

'I don't know.' She hurried out where little Jamie wanted a drink of water.

The sky had turned grey and a wind was coming up. Leaves and paper were blown around, and the piece of awning attached to the verandah was flapping as if trying to tear loose.

Alice looked across at Granny Johnston's hut for comfort, for support, but the door was shut and there was no light on.

By the time Alice left the shanty site the rain was pouring down. She had put on her best dress; she had told Jimmy she didn't want him to be ashamed of her when she met that bloke. He had said nothing, just looked at her in his quiet way.

She drove round the back of the hotel and parked the car. The place was quite old; the main building was made of red bricks which had once been painted white, but the paint was flaking. Numerous small weatherboard buildings had been added, with corrugated iron roofs, and everything was decorated and pasted over with bill boards and posters advertising beer and cigarettes.

The rain showed no sign of stopping, and Alice sat in the car and steeled herself for the ordeal. She knew the place. Long ago, she and Cutler had come here for lunch once or twice. He hadn't worried in those days to be seen with an Aboriginal girl . . .

The back door opened and a drunk came staggering out and made for the toilets. He tried to go round the puddles, but he slipped and nearly fell and had to support himself against the car.

She saw with relief that he was a gubbah. She hated to see koories drunk.

When he had disappeared behind the brick wall of the 'Gents', she got out and made quickly for the door that led to the hall outside the dining room.

The waitress saw her and came to find out what she wanted. She was a friendly soul. When she went back to tell Cutler he had a visitor, she left the door ajar, and Alice could see him sitting there with two men from the local Council. So it wasn't just her he'd come to visit. She wondered if he'd come to talk to them about the shanty site, or whether he was here for some personal reason: she remembered that he'd once bought some land here in the area – very beautiful, with a creek running through it, and good trees. It had been quite cheap, and they had thought then that one day they'd retire here . . .

Alice turned away from the door and stared at a notice board on the wall. She could hear voices raised in the public bar, and the clatter of plates and cutlery being washed in the kitchen.

She didn't know how long she stood there, waiting, feeling that all this was happening to someone else.

And then there was a voice behind her: 'Hello, Alice . . .'

She turned: there he was, dressed in casual clothes, grinning a little awkwardly. That's how he had sometimes looked at her twenty years ago.

Her face was cold and still.

He cleared his throat. 'I've booked a room; we can talk in private there . . .' He took a key from his pocket and walked up the stairs, never expecting her to refuse.

She forced herself to follow him. Why did she have to meet him under his conditions? Why should they talk in a dingy room in a country pub? This made everything look cheap. But she pushed aside her anger. What did it matter? All she wanted now was to know about her daughter. Nothing else was that important.

She walked erect, her head high.

He stopped in front of a door, unlocked it, threw it open, and walked in.

The room was small and shabby, the furniture drab and old. His business suit was lying on the bed, together with his tie, his briefcase.

She entered, and he shut the door. He didn't know how to begin the conversation, and she did nothing to make it easier. 'Sit down,' he said, 'sit down...' She remained standing, aloof and silent.

'You haven't changed,' he said at last, genially. She did not bother to reply.

He made for the small fridge and offered her a drink. She shook her head. He poured himself a Scotch. 'You're sure you don't want anything? Gin and tonic? Vermouth?' He'd stocked up on miniature bottles for the occasion.

She once more shook her head.

'Small world, eh?' he said, after he had fortified himself. 'Please do sit down,' he said again.

She ignored the invitation.

'Oh, by the way,' he assumed his jovial official tone, 'I'm confident we'll be able to do something about better housing soon for you people here ... might involve some shifting, though.'

'Is it true you have my daughter?'

He froze and stared into his glass, as if he thought the question would go away if he didn't respond to it.

'It is, isn't it?' Her voice was flat.

He tossed down the remainder of his drink. Her eyes were fixed on him.

She found it hard to speak, almost choking on the rage that threatened to overpower her. 'You stole her from me! – You!' she spat the word. Her eyes were burning in her face. 'It was you! How could you? How could you do this to anyone?'

Her voice had risen and she was close to breaking down as she remembered the despair, the frustration, worry, all the anger she had felt. She remembered the impassive expression on the faces of all the clerks and social workers she had questioned and pleaded with. 'I looked for her for years! No one would tell me anything! I thought that she had died!

He stared into his glass, and she felt she could not get through to him. 'Didn't you ever think of me? Didn't you think I loved my daughter?'

154

'You didn't care for her! You dumped her on old Granny!' His voice rose in self-defence.

'I had to go to work!' She was almost inarticulate. 'We would have starved!'

'Well, at least I didn't shirk my responsibilities – which most of the blokes would have done.' He sounded like the injured party. 'I didn't want a child!'

So now it was all her fault. She stood, fists clenched, finding it hard to breathe. She could feel her heart thumping in her breast.

'Look, Alice,' he tried to sound calm and reasonable, 'what's past is past, we cannot change what happened.'

'No,' she thought, 'you can never give me back those years I could have had with my daughter ...'

'Anyway, we've given her a proper home, a good education. What did you have to offer?'

She stared at him, then said icily: 'You sent me a telegram. What do you want from me?'

Cutler ran his hand across his face. 'Look, Alice,' he said at last, 'in the past I wasn't in a position to give you any money; I'd like you to accept some now ...' He fumbled for his wallet.

She was too stunned to move, to say anything.

'There's not much here' – he sounded apologetic – 'just about three hundred dollars, but I can let you have more ...'

'What's the money for? I don't want your money!'

He stood, holding the notes in his outstretched hand.

'... Are you trying to buy me off?' She could not believe that he would sink so low. But then, what else could he mean? 'What are you afraid of, Doug? That I'll blackmail you?'

'No, no,' he said hastily, and withdrew his hand. 'I know you're not the type.'

'All I want is to see my daughter.'

Cutler frowned and put away his wallet. He couldn't let it happen. He could see his whole life go to pieces.

'I don't think that's a good idea,' he said carefully. 'Look, she's leading a good life; Joy and I have brought her up ... Why upset the girl? You've got nothing in common, you and her.'

'Haven't we?'

There was a pause. Outside the rain was still coming down and drumming against the window. People were brawling in the bar.

'I'm her mother.'

'Look, Alice . . .' he tried to sound calm, reasonable. 'You'd both be disappointed. She's not like you expect. She's like a white girl. She's not really Aboriginal.'

Alice flared again. 'Yes, she is! Her mother is – and you didn't mind that once! And my mother is, and my mother's mother, and her mother before that. That makes her Aboriginal right back to the time of the Ancestors!'

Cutler looked at her; he couldn't find the words to explain his reasons without upsetting her even more. He felt guilty, but at the same time he felt what he had done was justified.

'I want you to bring my daughter here to meet me, Doug.' Alice turned to the door. She was very quiet now. 'I'm going to see her, Doug. And if you don't arrange it, I'll come and see her at your home.'

And she walked out, shutting the door quietly behind her.

Lo-Arna was coming home from a party at Nick Rowley's place. He was a fellow student, a friend at uni. It had been a fancy-dress do: 'Come as what you'd like to be'. What a thing to ask; it meant revealing something of yourself you'd really want to keep a secret – that is, if you took it seriously. Joy had suggested she dress up in a sarong and go as a Polynesian, but that, after all, was what she *was* anyway. She had decided she'd go as something that was too ludicrous to be taken as a hint of her real dreams. She went as Barbarella, in a crazy, scanty space costume.

When she came home at about three in the morning, she saw the light was on in the master bedroom. Good grief! Had they waited up for her? Would she get a lecture? She didn't really care: she'd had a few drinks, and she felt like floating up the stairs.

Her father appeared on the landing, a black shadow against the light of the bedside lamp.

'Ann, is that you?'

Who else could it be? She giggled. 'No, Dad, it's the fairy godmother . . .'

But he was not amused. 'Come in here, please, I want to talk to you.'

As she entered the bedroom, she saw at once something was very wrong. Joy was sitting on the bed; she was staring at the carpet, and her face was white and drawn.

Her father, too, looked strained. It was as if someone had died and they had just heard the news and didn't know how to tell.

'Ann,' her father said at last, 'what I'm about to say is far from easy. It concerns all of us. You in particular. It's time you knew the truth . . .'

He cleared his throat, forced himself to speak. 'I think Joy and I have always treated you like our own daughter . . .' He paused, then said abruptly: 'Well, you are. You are my daughter.'

Joy moaned, as if in pain.

Lo-Arna was bewildered, speechless.

'You understand what I'm saying? You are my daughter. Not an adopted child.'

She looked at Joy, who buried her face in her hands. Who then was her mother?

Her father continued rapidly: 'Your mother's a woman called Alice Wilson. And she's Aboriginal.'

Joy pressed her hands against her ears, cringing. 'It's all so ugly, ugly, ugly . . .'

Lo-Arna looked from Joy to her father: he was like someone who had just made a shameful, terrible confession and was looking for forgiveness. He stretched out his hand to touch her, but she pulled back and ran from the room.

She didn't know how she got down the stairs and into her little car. She could hear her father call her name, but she wasn't going back. Not ever.

Then she was driving, her father's words echoing inside her head: 'Aboriginal. Alice Wilson, and she's Aboriginal . . .' He – her father! Her real father! She felt betrayed by everyone.

She was going along the freeway. There was hardly any traffic on the road, and she went very fast. She didn't care.

Behind her was another car. She felt as if it was after her, so she went faster still. Inside her there was so much rage, so much confusion – she thought she could not bear it; that something would snap in her brain and that would be the end.

She found herself on the boulevard along the river. She couldn't remember when and where she'd left the freeway. There was a lot of mist, and she could hardly see the road. The headlights seemed to bounce off the mist, unable to penetrate it. The streetlights were as weak as candles.

She had slowed down. She felt scared and lost. There was nothing here against which she could vent her anger, nothing she could escape from. She was caught in this eerie, silent isolation.

In front of the car, suddenly out of the mist, there was a dog. He stood head-on, ears pricked, fixed in her lights. He looked like a dingo. She swerved and hit the nearest pole. Not hard, but hard enough to buckle the bonnet, and to make her bump her head.

She did not know how long she sat there, her eyes closed, leaning back. She didn't know if she had lost consciousness, but there seemed to be a gap between the appearance of the dog and this timeless moment.

Through the mist she saw the glow of a small fire. Gradually she could make out a woman sitting next to it. She was dressed in black. The face turned to look at her. It was the woman of her memory with her white hair, dark eyes. Lo-Arna could see now she was Aboriginal.

Lo-Arna shut her eyes, as if to blot out the sight. When she opened them, the woman and the fire had both vanished.

Strangely, this mystery calmed her, and she was able to think again. One thing was certain: she was not going home. She could not face her father.

The car was undrivable. She left the key, banged the door shut, and began to walk. She would go to Nick. She could think of nowhere else.

She suddenly became conscious of her outfit: Barbarella! What if someone saw her! She began to run, not sure how soon it would be dawn. She ran through the deserted streets, past warehouses and factories and cyclone fences and small weather-board cottages, and every time she saw the headlights of a car she ducked for cover behind garbage bins, doorways, fences.

Away from the river the mist dispersed, and she found she was not too far from Nick's place. She must have headed for it without thinking when she was driving.

He lived in a small old house with a tiny backyard. The lights were on, the door was open, but almost all the guests' cars had gone, and it was quiet.

Nick, still in his Groucho Marx costume complete with mous-tache, was stacking empty bottles. At first he stared at her, about to crack a joke, but then his expression changed.

'What's happened?'

She didn't answer. Now that she was safe, everything around her began to spin. She felt him take her by the shoulders. His face was close to hers.

'Ann! What's the matter?' He was alarmed.

She began to retch, and she just made it to the toilet where she was sick.

After that she still didn't answer any questions. She couldn't see any sense in talking. All she wanted was to do nothing, be nothing, think nothing.

Nick made some coffee, and they sat on the old straight kitchen chairs in the small pool of light that came from the crazy paper lantern above the table. Lo-Arna nursed the cup between her hands but didn't drink, or speak.

Nick tried another tack: he spoke, pretending nothing unusual was going on. He talked about the party, about uni, about world affairs, not at all sure how to handle the situation. At the same time he wondered if he should call a doctor, the police . . .

As he talked and talked, Lo-Arna felt resentment building up inside her – a deep, futile resentment against life, against fate that had made her Aboriginal. She felt herself raging against herself and knew at the same time that it was no use. She was what she was. Every single cell of her, each particle of blood. Her brain, her mind. She felt contaminated by some dreadful disease that permeated her whole being.

'I'll take you home,' she heard him say.

'I'm not going.' He seemed so smug to her.

'I'll get a taxi.' He was relieved some contact had been made.

She raised her voice. 'I'm not going home!' She sounded like a stubborn, desperate child. 'I'm staying here!'

'Why?' He leant forward, almost thrust his face into Lo-Arna's. 'Just tell me one good reason why you want to stay in a dump like this?'

She raised her eyes for the first time, wondering what he would say when he was told the truth. He was exasperated. 'You took off from here like a virginal princess bent on some outer galaxy, and you come back a black blob of doom!'

'Do you know what I am?' she said in a voice so low it was barely audible.

Nick waited.

'I'm a boong. A bloody Abo.'

The words seemed to float in the air.

Nick for a moment could not believe he had heard correctly. But then a load came off his chest. He gave a quick laugh: 'Well – so what? Congratulations!'

She leapt to her feet and hit him hard across the face.

He stared, and slowly rubbed his cheek.

For a moment everything was still. Then she threw up her hands, covered her face and began to cry in a high-pitched, keening sound. He got up and took her in his arms and held her close while she wept as if her heart would break.

'I don't see what you're so upset about,' he said quietly, truthfully, when she had calmed herself a little.

'It's all so ugly, ugly, ugly...' Lo-Arna could still hear Joy's words ringing in her ears.

'Why? How? You are still you! Nothing's changed! You haven't changed!'

It was so glib, so trite. 'Shut up,' she said.

Nick tried to sort things out. 'How on earth did you get this information in the middle of the night? I mean... how do you know it's true?'

'My father told me.'

Nick was staggered. 'You met your real dad?'

'Met?' She was bitter. 'Met? ... I've lived in his house for eighteen years! Oh, he makes me sick! That hypocrite! That 'Mr Clean'! That nice charming proper gentleman! He never told me! Never ...'

For a while they sat in silence. Around them was the debris of the party: paper streamers snaking across the floor, limp on the furniture. There were dirty glasses and used plates, ashtrays full of butts, the stale smell of tobacco. In the next room, in the semi-dark, someone was sleeping on the floor, his fancy dress awry.

At last Nick gently took her face into his hands and made her look at him. 'Listen,' he said quietly, 'this is not the end of everything. You've had a shock. You'll get over it. You'll work things out. I know you will ...'

She did not reply.

'I'll take you home.'

'You want to get rid of me,' she said tonelessly.

'You know I don't.' He stroked her hair. 'I don't care what you are ... Polynesian princess, Madame Galactica, a wog, a chink, a boong, a bloody ocker ...'

She gave him a bitter smile. 'That's big of you,' she said. 'To you I am acceptable ... but not to me.'

She did not resist when he put her into his car. She sat in it like a zombie when he drove her home. Back at the house she did not take any notice of Joy and her father as she walked past them up to her room. There she lay on her bed, staring at the ceiling, till the sun was up. Then she had a shower. She scrubbed herself till she was red and sore, and still she felt unclean.

When she finally came down to have a glass of orange juice, she found her father and his wife having breakfast, though it was very late. Nobody knew what to say, and they avoided looking at each other – till Joy broke the silence, just as Lo-Arna was about to leave the room again.

'Have you ... told Nick?' she asked.

Lo-Arna paused. If she said she had, there might be more questions. So she simply shook her head. Joy was relieved. 'That's good,' she said, 'no one need ever know ...'

Lo-Arna did not go to uni. She stayed home, unable to find the will, the energy, to do anything constructive. Her future, once so bright, so full of possibilities and challenges, now stretched out in front of her like a wasteland under a grey sky. She vaguely considered leaving home, but even that seemed pointless: she would never be able to escape from her own self.

She noticed with bitter satisfaction how the events had upset her father's cosy, comfortable life. He looked worn and tense. At the same time it added to her sense of worthlessness to see how anxious he was to hide 'the indiscretion' he had committed twenty years ago. And she could not work out why he had adopted her: she must have been a constant reminder of her mother. Perhaps he had felt guilt, and pity. Lo-Arna hated pity. She found it hard now to believe that he had ever loved her. If he had, would he not stand up for what he'd done? Instead he was on the run. He said he was sick of his job, the rat-race. He wanted to retire, buy himself a small farm, and live on the land.

He and Joy had heated arguments. In a way Lo-Arna had to admire her – her strength, resilience, determination. She had decided that life had to go on as it had before. She had known that Lo-Arna was Aboriginal, but had seen this as a challenge. But she had not known her husband was the father. Now she thought she had been used by her husband to bring up his illegitimate child; she had been exploited. She was entitled to compensation: to lead the kind of life she wanted. And that was life in the city, or at least close to it.

Lo-Arna was lying in the garden when she heard the postman's whistle. Slowly she got up and meandered to the letter box. She took out the mail and on the way to the house she cast a cursory glance at it. Her heart missed a beat: there was a yellow envelope; it was addressed to Lo-Arna Cutler, c/o Aboriginal Women's Project Centre, at an address in Richmond. 'Please forward' was written on it. 'Lo-Arna': it must be her own name.

Lo-Arna carried it into the house with the other letters, and then she stood in the kitchen and held it in her hand and stared at it. She was afraid to open it. She felt Joy watching her, and she couldn't help thinking that, if Joy had gone to collect the mail, she would not have received it.

That made her take it to her room. She did not want anyone to see her when she opened it. It felt as if there was something else in it, not just a letter.

She shut the door and sat down on her bed. She looked at the writing. She was sure it was her mother's hand. She was holding something that had been touched by her . . . It almost burnt her fingers.

At last she opened it.

A weird thing slid into her hand: after a brief shock she realized it was a string of eucalyptus seeds. With it was an old photograph, a little faded. It showed a small girl with a big smile on the knees of a dark woman who also smiled.

On the back of it was written: 'Kyewong 1961, Alice and Lo-Arna.' And in another handwriting – the same as on the envelope – 'To Lo-Arna, with love from her mother'.

Tears welled up in Lo-Arna's eyes and ran down her face. She cried about this woman who was her mother, and she cried about herself. She cried that she was ever born. Somehow the tears seemed to wash away some of the harshness of her despair, as water does when it runs over rocks, softening the edge.

She put the necklace and the photo in her desk and locked it. Then she washed her face; she didn't want Joy to know she had been crying. Later she went downstairs, and when Joy asked her about the letter, she said quite casually that there had been a necklace in it, made of eucalyptus seeds. Joy said 'That's nice . . .' and they didn't talk about it anymore. But in the air there were many unspoken things.

In the evening, when her father came home from work, Lo-Arna overheard Joy tell him worriedly that the Aboriginal woman had been in touch. She could see a problem: what if a whole gang of them turned up? What would the neighbours say? They might instal themselves in the house and garden, claiming the land belonged to them.

Cutler, too, felt uneasy, but he tried not to show it. It was unlikely anything like that would happen. The important thing was not to encourage them. And – if the worst came to the worst – there was always the police. They stopped talking when they noticed Lo-Arna.

She had been up to her room many times that day. She had looked at the photograph, the inscription. 'Lo-Arna' – what did it mean? She tried to come to terms with the sound of it: 'Lo-Arna'. She stared into the mirror, and a stranger stared back at her, red-eyed and wan and filled with apprehension and uncertainty. She'd have to learn to live with her. She longed for the days when she did not know her origins, when she had been free to dream. 'My Polynesian princess' Joy had sometimes called her smilingly . . .

She picked up the necklace, fingered it, but could not make herself put it on. It was like a living thing, a small snake. She felt there was some magic in it, very old, and if she wore it she would be transformed into something she did not want to be. Again she picked up the photograph and peered at the woman's face, trying to make it come to life. She could see some beauty in her now. And there was something in her smile that made one think she cared for her little girl, that she was proud of her . . .

She would ask her father.

Joy had gone to bed, and she knew he was alone in the living room, listening to music. It would be good to talk. The silence about what had happened made life intolerable, not easier – as Joy had said. Her father – she had to admit – had always been good to her. He had helped her with her studies, he had encouraged her. He seemed proud of her sometimes . . .

When she walked into the room she found him lying on the couch, eyes shut. The light from the standard lamp cast a warm glow on his face. She was surprised to see him look so vulnerable. His mind seemed far away. She felt she shouldn't be there – intruding on his privacy.

She stood, not sure what to do. He suddenly noticed he was not alone, stared at her blankly for a moment, then hastily sat up, looking guilty – as if she had caught him thinking something she was not supposed to know.

'Good God,' he said with a light laugh, 'you gave me quite a shock . . . Why aren't you in bed?'

She sat down on the carpet.

'Tell me about my mother.'

She was surprised that it had been quite easy to say that word.

She waited.

164

'What do you want to know?' he said at last.

'What was she like?'

He got up to turn down the volume of the music, and she felt that he was stalling. It was true. A moment ago he had remembered some of the days with Alice. They had gone swimming in the river. The wattles had been in bloom, their golden yellow had lit up the countryside, and all the problems of the world were far away. They had made love on the river bank. Alice had been so full of life, so generous, so honest . . . It had not been easy to stop seeing her. It had been a sacrifice he had had to make . . . for his parents' sake, for his career.

'There isn't much to tell,' he said. 'She was a nursing aide at the District Hospital. In those days Aboriginal girls were getting into nursing . . .'

She searched his face.

'Were you . . . fond of her?'

She was afraid to use the word 'love'.

He sat down on the couch and nodded. 'Oh yes,' he said – and it seemed he spoke honestly. 'I was very fond of her. She was different from all the other girls I knew. Full of fun. Uncomplicated.' He looked at his daughter. 'She had lovely eyes, like you . . .'

She did not like him saying this. It seemed a superficial reason for loving anyone.

'If you loved her,' she said abruptly, 'why didn't you marry her?'

For a few moments he was silent. 'Well . . . I don't think she expected it,' he said at last. 'Anyway, it would not have worked. She would have felt out of place in a white society.'

Lo-Arna thought of the photograph, and there was a lump in her throat when she asked: 'Didn't she mind when you took me away?'

'Oh no, no.' The answer came too quickly. 'I'd say she was relieved. She'd have had trouble looking after you, giving you a decent education . . .' He paused. 'Anyway, there was another bloke she was interested in . . .'

Lo-Arna looked at her father, and he looked back at her, with an expression of total sincerity. She wondered if she could ever trust him again. 'To Lo-Arna, with love from her mother' – she saw the writing clearly in front of her.

'Did she . . . ever want to see me . . . ?' Her voice was shaky.

'No.' Again the answer was very quick. 'Never came near you, Ann. She wasn't interested, really . . .' He sounded sorry.

'. . . Wasn't she?'

He shook his head, with that same regretful expression on his face.

She got up, made for the door.

'You aren't thinking of getting in touch with her?'

She turned. He stood there, watching her anxiously. She was surprised that he had thought she would. She had not yet considered it.

He spoke urgently, warningly. 'You'd be expected to give up everything you've got. Share everything. You'd cause a lot of envy. We'd have the whole tribe on our doorstep if you let them know how you live . . .'

The words poured out of him as he found one reason after the other. 'And they'd want you to fight their battles – because you've got an education! You are presentable. Don't throw your life away on the militant blacks!'

Lo-Arna didn't know what to say. Why did he care what she did with her life?

She left the room without reassuring him. She needed time to think.

Alice was waiting. Waiting for Lo-Arna. For some response from her – however small. She didn't know how many times a day she looked towards the entrance to the site, willing a car to drive up and a girl to get out who was her daughter. She tried to picture her. She wondered what her voice was like. Was she kind? Generous? Was she arrogant, aloof? What would they say to each other? What could you say to a daughter you had never known, who had grown up in a different world?

Cars came, but none bringing Lo-Arna. There were letters, but not one from her daughter.

Alice often sat with Granny Johnston. The old woman suffered with her. Now and then she'd take her hand reassuringly, like someone who sits with an invalid who is waiting to get well.

Alice had at last told Jimmy about Lo-Arna. He had guessed that she had once been in love with Cutler. It hadn't worried him that much; it had happened a long time before he knew Alice. But he was hurt that she had not trusted him enough to tell him the whole truth. He had said little, but their relationship was marred, and she did not know when he would come to understand why she had been so secretive.

One day she was down by the river, by herself. Here she found more peace than in any other place. It was morning, and the children were at school. Magpies were carolling; a kookaburra sat perched on the lowest branch of a tall tree and studied her, head cocked to one side. A stream of tiny ants made their way across a decaying log. The air was filled with the scent of eucalypts. She took off her shoes and felt the earth under her bare feet. She put her hand against the rough bark of a tree, and it gave her strength.

And then she heard the sound of an engine starting up, quite close. For a moment she froze and listened, and then she realized what it meant. She put on her shoes and scrambled up the bank, back to the shanty site.

The dozer had arrived. It was spattered with dirt and mud, but its blade was clean and gleaming. It stood there, throbbing, waiting, ready to do its job. Behind it was the loader that had brought it, and next to it the car of the shire engineer. People had assembled and the air was thick with tension. The health inspector, a stout, pink, balding man, was leaning against the bonnet, arms crossed in front of his chest. 'You've had fair warning,' he said above the noise of the dozer. 'We've got our orders.' The shire engineer stood beside him. He made a sweeping gesture: 'These constructions are against Council regulations, for a start. You've turned this place into a rubbish dump!'

'And you've turned the whole of Australia into a rubbish dump!' Jimmy shouted. He was angrier than Alice had ever seen.

She looked around, and she felt a deep anguish: this small patch of soil with its few gums and shrubs, its river bank, its tall, slender grass blown by the wind . . . it was a remnant of where the Nyari once had lived. She came from here. She, her mother, her mother's mother, her mother before that. And Lo-Arna. She, too, came from this land. It was her blood, her flesh, her sinews. How could a whitefeller understand?

She saw that Granny had begun to pack and went to help her. She picked up the old rocking chair, and the cardboard boxes containing letters and photographs of bygone battles, and the few clothes she had, and put it all into the caravan. She didn't think the dozer would touch the caravan: it wasn't an 'unauthorized building'; it had wheels.

In the background the dozer had begun to move. Slowly, inexorably, it made its way towards the old car body that had served the children as a cubby house. Some women now began to gather their belongings, trying to save what they could in the short time that was left: pots and pans, food and clothes, some furniture. Most of the men were still arguing. The police had arrived, and now and then Alice could hear a few words above the noise the dozer made.

'You don't want us to live anywhere!' a man shouted, and in his voice there was the sound of all those who had been dispossessed. It was the same despair, the same feeling of impotent, hopeless rage.

The dozer rumbled on. Some of the people ran in front of it to bar its way. It was like a war. The police pulled them away. Alice could have cried with compassion and fierce anger. She felt a searing hate for all those responsible for their plight. She thought of Cutler, smug somewhere in his office, removed from everything that was happening here. She could picture him in a neat suburban home, telling Lo-Arna that her mother was not good enough, a drunk, a slut, who lived in squalor and had to be swept away like garbage.

The dozer crunched the humpies, gouging out between collapsing walls things which had been cherished by the occupants: a few soft cushions, a framed picture, a kero-stove, a hot-water bottle, a child's chair . . .

By now most of the people stood in a group and watched, numb and still, as things that were their very own were laid bare for all the world to see. Granny was leaning against Alice, and tears were running down her face. Tears, Alice knew, for white as well as black.

The dozer was remorseless. Some women couldn't bear the sight any longer, and moaned and turned away.

'This one's got to go, too!' The engineer shouted and pointed at Granny Johnston's hut.

'That one?' the driver yelled. He was Italian, and he had never done this kind of thing before.

'Got to go!'

The driver pointed at Granny Johnston. 'That woman like my grandmother!' he called out.

'Bugger your grandmother!'

The driver suddenly turned off the engine and climbed down. 'You do your own dirty work,' he said, 'I finish. Finito!' He walked off.

There was an outburst of clapping and some cheering, but there was no joy in it.

The engineer was fuming. The driver of the loader knew how to work the dozer, and he swung himself onto the machine and started it again.

And so Granny Johnston's hut went, too – with its small verandah, the sarsparilla still clinging to the posts, with its vegetable garden in which the tomatoes were just turning red.

That same day the people from the shanty site went to pay a visit to Doug Cutler in his office. Only Jimmy stayed behind, with little Jamie and with Granny. He didn't want to leave the caravan unattended: some smart Alec from the Council might have towed it away.

Val Pearce was leading the delegation: men, women, youngsters, children – even babies. When they came out of the lifts on the twentieth floor, the receptionist behind the desk nearly choked on a lolly at the sight of the invasion.

Val walked up to her and demanded to see Doug Cutler. She was told he was in conference. 'Tell him to come out,' Val said. 'He's got a conference here. I'm Val Pearce. He knows me.'

The receptionist disappeared. Through the windows you could see the skyscrapers and the tops of older houses. One of them had a children's playground on it, but it looked abandoned.

The koories sat down on the chairs and on the carpet, their kids, their string bags, their boxes and their bundles next to them. Alice's heart was with them, but at the same time she felt detached: this was the day on which she would meet her daughter.

She saw a young fellow come back with the receptionist. He was very neat: nice suit and tie, short wavy hair, polished face.

'What's going on?' he said, and tried to sound in charge.

'We're not speaking to pencil sharpeners,' Val said briskly. 'We want to speak to Cutler.'

The young man was peeved. He threatened to call the police.

'You tell Cutler to come out, or we'll rip the pants off you and send you back without them,' one of the women said, and she looked as if she meant it. The young man departed.

Then Cutler came. He caught sight of Alice, but managed to look concerned and friendly, and he put on quite a show of indignation when he heard that the Council had moved the dozers in. He would see what he could do. With that, he thought, everyone would be satisfied and go home. They reminded him they had no home to go to. Val informed him that all the koories would be staying at his office till he had found them accommodation. There was a hint of panic in his face, but he organized tea, coffee, sandwiches, and he took Val and Alice into his office where he did some phoning.

Alice looked at him, at his pinched, sallow face, ordering this and that in his kingdom of glass doors and pot plants, and it struck her suddenly that he was trapped. Trapped by his sense of values, by his world. Once he had tried to break free, but he hadn't had the guts to do it. That's why he had stolen her daughter from her: she was a symbol, the embodiment of what he had forfeited. It was clear to her now, but she felt no pity.

170

He managed to get them temporarily fixed up at the Batman Migrant Hostel. 'With the Vietnamese . . . all ethnics together, eh?' Val said sarcastically. Then she went to tell the others, who had made themselves at home in the boardroom and the kitchen next to it, and in the waiting room.

Val drove Alice to Cutler's house. Alice didn't speak. She sat and stared through the window – at the street her daughter would have walked many times, at the trees her daughter saw every day.

They pulled up outside the house. For a moment Alice found it hard to move, to get out of the car. Her limbs felt as though they didn't belong to her.

She looked at the house. It was large and painted white, and surrounded by a high brick wall. There was a wooden gate with iron hinges. The place looked like a fortress on its small plot of land.

They walked through the gate. Alice had been sure that it would be locked and barred, but it had given way. They walked through the garden, past the well-kept lawn, the flowering roses and rhododendrons. A car was parked in the open garage. Alice and Val went to the front door, and Val rang the bell.

They waited.

Nothing happened.

Val rang the bell again. There was no sign of life.

Val tried to peer through the panel of coloured glass next to the door, but she couldn't see anything. Then she led the way around the house into the back garden. Perhaps someone was outside and had not heard the bell. She was determined to make this mission a success.

Alice followed a few steps behind. She was sure that Cutler had phoned Lo-Arna and had warned her of the possibility of her coming. She looked at the swimming pool, at the air mattress floating on it, at the swinging floral garden seat, at the shrubs, at the kabana. She could sense her daughter's presence. She felt that her eyes were watching her from a window. She touched the top of the garden chair where Lo-Arna's head must have rested many times. She wanted to call out, to shout her daughter's name – but she kept silent.

A lawn mower started up not far away.

The doors and windows of the house remained shut; the place took on a deserted look – as if no one was living there, and no one would live there again.

'Let's go,' Alice said quietly. 'There's no one home . . .'

Lo-Arna stood transfixed as she watched her mother from behind the curtain of an upstairs window. She saw her go round the corner, dressed in a simple frock, carrying a bag, vulnerable yet with a simple dignity. She saw her go out through the gate in the high brick wall; she heard car doors slam, an engine start and a car drive off. All the while one part of her had wanted to call out to her, make her stop, while the other was rigid with prejudice and fear.

That night Lo-Arna could not sleep. She tossed and turned, and every time she shut her eyes she saw the silhouette of her mother behind the coloured glass of the front door. She saw her move around the house like a dark ghost that had come to claim her, haunt her.

She turned on the light. It was four o'clock. She got dressed. Then she unlocked the drawer of her desk and took out the string of seeds. Fighting her apprehension, she slipped it over her head and let it settle around her neck.

And then she walked out of the room to see her father and his wife.

Her father was the first to jerk awake. He sat up, startled, and turned on the bedside lamp.

She stood at the foot of the bed. 'I'm going to Kyewong. I'm going to see my mother.'

He found it hard to cope; he was still drowsy. 'Now?'

'Yes.'

Joy stirred and propped on one elbow.

'But why?' He couldn't believe all this was happening.

'I want to meet her.'

Joy moaned. 'Oh, Ann, it can only hurt you . . .'

'She came here yesterday, and I couldn't face her. I didn't have the guts to call out to her!' Joy tried to say something, but Lo-Arna cut her off. 'That woman – she's my mother! She carried me inside her – and I couldn't make myself simply meet her!' The words poured out of her. 'I want to know her, I want to touch her. I want to listen to what she has to say . . .'

They tried to dissuade her. They told her she was full of ideals, wanting to do what she thought was right. She could never really know her mother or her people. She imagined it was romantic because of legends she had heard about the Dreamtime. Things were different now; they reminded her of all the social problems – that the Aborigines had the highest jail rate, there were drinking problems, health problems . . .

Lo-Arna did not budge. 'My mother looked fine to me,' she said.

By this time Joy was wide awake. 'Listen,' she said, 'I've never asked you for anything. Now I do. Don't go. Don't, for my sake . . .'

Lo-Arna looked away.

'How can you walk out on us!' Joy was suddenly close to tears.

'I'm not. I'm not forgetting what you have done for me . . .' Lo-Arna despaired that they would ever understand.

'We know what's best,' Cutler said abruptly. 'You've got to trust us, Ann . . .'

'How can I – when you've lied to me all these years!'

Her father didn't know what to say.

'And you want me to go on lying! You are making me feel ashamed of myself! Why should I feel ashamed?' Lo-Arna choked back her own tears.

Joy flung herself back into her pillow. 'You're making far too much of this,' she said bitterly, 'and you're taking a dreadful risk.'

'I know.'

Joy's voice was now cold: 'There's one thing, one condition. If you make contact, don't involve us. Do you understand?'

Lo-Arna looked hard at Joy, and at her father who had turned away. For a few moments there was silence.

'Yes,' she said, and went out.

The first light of dawn was in the sky as Lo-Arna left the city. She drove past oil refineries and factories out into the country towards Kyewong.

The land was flat and bare, broken by few trees; in the distance, black against the sky, there was a line of hills.

She had the feeling that the wheels of the car were turning without her directing them. She was being sucked into this space before her, into the landscape – faster, faster, and there was nothing she could do to stop.

Then the sky turned a pale gold, and through the distant haze on the horizon she could see the huge orange disc of the sun come over the mountain range – powerful, mysterious. Never before had she seen the rising of the sun with a mind so alert and so receptive.

She saw the rays touch the mountain tops, the trees, the plain; she saw colours come to life, and she was filled with awe. Her spirit seemed to return to the dawn of time and she felt a sudden deep understanding of the magnificence of creation, of the universe.

She left the freeway and turned into the road to Kyewong.

The milk bar was just opening its door when she drove up. She asked the woman where the Aborigines lived. The woman looked her up and down, then said: 'They've all gone. The dozers got them out.'

Lo-Arna stared at her. It could not be true. Her mother must be there!

'Where is the place?' Her voice was trembling.

The woman pointed up the road, told her to take the first track after the turn-off to the rubbish tip.

Lo-Arna got back into the car. She didn't care what the woman thought. She left the main street behind and drove along the gravel road, past paddocks, past groves of eucalyptus trees.

By now the sun had fully risen. In the sky before her she could see a majestic bird soaring, wings spread wide. Below, the trees were swaying in gusts of wind, and a willy-willy was dancing on the track ahead. The bird seemed motionless, divorced from the restiveness beneath.

She found the track to the shanty site and slowed the car. Her mouth was dry, she could feel her heart thumping against her ribs. She wanted to see the place where her mother had been living. She wanted to walk on the same soil.

At last she reached the clearing. It looked like a battle field. The dozer had left deep scars in the earth, and here and there some things were scattered that had been missed: a broken chair, some firewood, a bag, an old shovel. In one corner there was a heap of corrugated iron sheets waiting to be taken to the tip.

Opposite, in front of some manna gums, there was the only sign of habitation: an old caravan. A man was dismantling a kind of verandah that had been attached to it. Now he turned and watched as she approached.

She stopped the car, felt herself getting out.

The man was very dark, and he was dressed in working clothes. His questioning expression became a long probing look, as she approached, but then his face began to thaw.

'Excuse me,' Lo-Arna said, 'can you tell me where I could find Alice Wilson?'

The man smiled. It was a smile from his eyes, not his lips. 'I'll get her for you,' he said. 'She's gone down to the river. You wait in the caravan . . .'

He walked off quickly, and then broke into a run – a swift, smooth, even run.

Lo-Arna looked around her. Thanks to the trees that formed a barrier with a line of shrubs, the wind here was powerless. Magpies sang as they picked their way through the place that had once sheltered the humpies of her people.

She looked at the entrance to the caravan, small and dark, beckoning her to enter. Almost against her will she did.

After the bright light outside she could at first see nothing. Then she realized that she was not alone. Someone was sitting in the shadows, watching her: an old woman, dressed in black, her hair white, like the clouds.

'So you've come home . . .' she said.

Lo-Arna shivered; she was involved in something that was awesome, inexplicable.

'I . . . don't think I'll wait,' she stammered. 'Will you please tell my mother I am sorry. I'll come back some other time . . .'

She turned and fled to her car. The engine started, she drove off. She began to cry – sorry for herself, her weakness, her fear.

And then she caught sight of someone in the rear-vision mirror. It was her mother running, calling, her arms reaching out through the stones and dust.

Afterword

Women of the Sun was first conceived as a series for television because it was the most direct way to bring Aboriginal life and thought into the homes of the general public. Apart from its contribution to setting the record straight about Australian Aboriginal history during the last 200 years, we wanted to involve as many members of the Aboriginal community as possible. Many white Australians have never met an Aborigine. One of the constant arguments we heard from potential producers and industry experts while we researched and wrote the series was that we would never find enough Aboriginal actors and actresses for it. The performances by Aboriginals in the series, most of who had never before appeared on television or film, should give them something to think about.

After the series had gone to air and the excitement had died down, the spirits of those who had been brought to life in the series refused to go away. Something else was needed. Something that made them permanent. That's why this book was written.

We dedicate it to all those who have struggled against great odds to keep alive the soul and culture of the people.

Hyllus Maris
Sonia Borg